BLIND RAFTERY

GOLDEN GOAT
THE POWER OF THE DOG
HANGMAN'S HOUSE
BROTHER SAUL
MESSER MARCO POLO
CRUSADE
THE WIND BLOWETH
THE FOOLISH MATRONS
CHANGELING
AN UNTITLED STORY
DESTINY BAY
IRELAND, THE ROCK WHENCE I WAS
   HEWN

BLIND RAFTERY

AND

HIS WIFE, HILARIA

BY

DONN BYRNE

LONDON
SAMPSON LOW, MARSTON & CO., LTD.

239683

MADE AND PRINTED IN GREAT BRITAIN BY
PURNELL AND SONS PAULTON (SOMERSET) AND LONDON

BLIND RAFTERY

CHAPTER I

As he sat there in the withdrawing-room of Patrick Lynch's inn, all the life, all the spirit of Galway was evident to him. He could sense the deep shadows of the room, and the May sunshine coming into it through the open windows, yellow as yellow wine. And to his nostrils came the salt Atlantic breeze, sweeping eastward from the islands of Aran. There were scents on the wind he could pick out one by one, the odour of the tarred ships riding at anchor in Galway Bay, the smell of the dulse, or Irish seaweed, with its pungent iodine flavour, and there was the pathetic lonely virginal scent of the little flowers that grow in the clefts of sea rocks, and of the honey-like heather, and the tang of the peat-smoke from the cottages, nostalgic as an ancient song.

Outside there was bustle and movement
He could hear the ring of his little mare's hoof
on the rain-washed cobble-stones, so impatient
she was to be on her way past the purple
Connemara mountains to the County of Clare.
Spring was coming in with the Atlantic
breezes, and bird and beast knew it, and man
and woman, too. There came to him the
sound of the voices without, an occasional tag
of Spanish from some sailor of Barcelona, a
peasant's soft liquid Erse, the voluble English
of the landlord and his people as they super-
vised the packing of his boxes on the led ponies.
The nervousness as the harp in its great
leather case was being lashed into position.

"Let you look out, now, Shamus Hennessy,
let you look out and you putting the harp o'
my heart on the beast's meagre back, for 'tis
how I'd rather have every rib in my body
broken nor a string of great Raftery's harp
gone wrong."

"Will you hold your whisht?"

"Easy now, easy now, Shamus Hennessy;
'tis not serving out pints of porter to the
tinkers of Galway you are, and you handling
that grand melodious thing!"

"Will you hold your whisht, man of the
house?"

"Will I hold your thrapple, if anything goes wrong."

Then came the sweet low laughter of Hilaria, like a wood-pigeon's crooning.

All the unrest of spring was on him, and he was thinking long for the moment when Hilaria would enter the room and tell him all was ready, and then walking beside her, her hand holding his privately, he would go down the stairs of Patrick Lynch's inn. She would lead him to the little mare's side and put the reins into his hands, and then, finding stirrup-iron himself, he would swing into the saddle as well as any man who had two eyes. And Hilaria would mount her sleek Spanish mule, and the Scots boy with the long legs and the hair cut like a Florentine page's would take hold of the lead reins of the packhorses. A piper of the town, some old man with loud silver-keyed pipes, would play a farewell in his honour, and the soft Connaught people would wish him luck. "God send you happy days, blind Raftery, and great songs to sing in them!"

And they would go then, Hilaria and he, on the long road that rambled southward to the seaport of Cork, over the heather-covered braes. The sun would rise on their left hand, and the warmth of it would come on them, soft as honey. Great drowsy Shannon would go with them part of their way, and listening one could hear the leap of the trout and the plunge of the otter, and the soft crooning of the river as its edge touched some little beach of rounded stones. And the mountains of Connemara on the right-hand side, one could feel their great golden entities. And all the scents of the flowers would come to him; the honeyed heather; the honest perfume of the humble flowers of the field, crimson-edged daisy and varnished buttercup; the modest violet with its fragrance like a soft note of the harp; and the high fine scent of the bog-flower. And on nights the moon would be up and they would ride on, the river singing beside them and the wind stirring the grasses, until one felt that accompanying them on the march were a host of the little people of the hills, the minute Irish fairies and the shy, light-footed leprechawns, called up by the soft magic of the moon.

And softer than any music would be the low contralto of Hilaria as she rode beside him on the Spanish jennet. Better than any eyes of his would be her eyes of wonder.

"O Raftery, there is a white cloud on the blue sky, and now it is under the sun, and

4

there is a purple cloak on the golden mountain-side."

"I can hear the mountain's silence," he would tell her.

"O Raftery, there is a kingfisher skimming the river. The sun is on his blue and white wings. He is close to the bank, dark Raftery."

"He is seeking his house, Hilaria. He has a tunnelled house in the river-bank."

"Raftery," she would say softly, "dusk is coming like a strange blue mist, and in the east is one small star."

"I can feel the ground drowsy as I ride over it, Hilaria," he said. "And the odour of the flowers comes less and less to me, as their petals close now the sun is down."

And they would come to an open beach on the sea-shore, where the green Atlantic came in on golden chiming sands. And there he would go in swimming, his only athletic accomplishment now he was blind. He would push off fearlessly into the great Atlantic, his powerful arms and shoulders sending him through the water like a salmon, keeping a course by the wind on his cheek, and turning intuitively inshore when he knew he was far enough out. And when he came to the shallows the Scots gillie would plunge in to guide him over the beach. When he was in the water his eyes were little lack to him. It was only on shore he had to be guided.

And at nightfall they would come to a village where a great house was, Norman noble's or Irish chief's, and at either was a great welcome put before him. And great respect, for a phrase of Raftery's might go down to one's grandchildren, and bring them pride. Or they might turn into some abbey of monks, and the father prior receive them with the hospitality of a viceroy, and when compline had been sung, Raftery would recite for the white-robed brethren some great poem of his, like "By the Green Woods of Truagh," marking the rhythm on the harp-strings. And the prior, who had been reared in courtly places, and he would discuss the great world until the small hours, while Hilaria slept. Or they might stay at a farm-house for the night, and the quiet peasantry would bring forward their children.

"Do you see this dark man, white children?"

"Yes, *mammy beg*, little mother, we see the dark man."

"It is great Raftery is in it, white children. When ye are old ye can say: 'With these eyes I have seen great Raftery.'"

"Great Raftery," they would lisp.

And Raftery would laugh and call for the harp to play a lullaby on it. He would hear their light feet coming closer and closer. He would put out a hand to take the nearest one.

"Would you like to play my harp, little brother?"

And the child in awe would put out a finger to touch the deep vibrating strings. And there would be tears in the eyes of the folk in the house.

He heard the quick spring of the gillie on the stairs; a low laughter, and a scuffle. One of Patrick Lynch's serving-girls was saying in a low voice:

"If I give you a kiss of my mouth, will you not ask me why?"

"Why shouldn't I?" And a little pause.

"'Tis because you are with great Raftery, tall lad."

"Reason enough," said the gillie.

They parted, for now came the soft tread of Hilaria on the stairs. The door opened, and the gentle lavender perfume of her came to Raftery where he sat. Her silken skirts rustled. She was like a flower coming into the room, some slight velvet flower.

"Raftery," she said. She put her hands on his broad shoulders. "Spring is here, and your horse is saddled, and there is a wind blowing from the south."

"Then we will go, Hilaria, we will go the road to the seaport of Cork."

"And where from there, Raftery?"

"Wherever the road is open, Hilaria, to the gay land of France, or High Germany, or the lowlands of Holland."

"Or black Africa?"

"Or the colonies of America, wherever there is an ear for a harp, or a heart open for a poem. Come, Hilaria, I am thinking long for the road."

"O Raftery, there is an old piper of the hills without, and he is playing 'Bundle and Go.' He is a very old man, and he says he has his health and his pipes, but there is only one trouble on him, that he will never see great Raftery any more. Don't give him gold or silver, my heart."

"What shall I give him, Hilaria?"

"Give him kind words, and the greeting of a brother, dear Raftery, and the generous hand-shake, so that he will go proudly piping to the gates of Heaven, when all his piping here is done."

CHAPTER II

Was it only two years ago he had been sitting here in this very town, sitting on a mooring-bitt on Galway pier, and people passing by had shown him no reverence but only a kindly familiarity, such as one might show a jockey or pugilist, and referring to him as "Poor Raftery, the poet"? And there was no dignity in his life, and only bitterness in his face. All the bustle of the seaport around him and none had time for him until evening, until the drinking-shops were open, and the edges of the harsh day were mellowed by wine. Here a ship bound for the Brazils was loading up with great blocks of Connemara marble, clouded green and black and silver, and here a little boat for Aran was loading with the dry peat squares for the islands' burning. Cut glass from Waterford and Ballycastle, lace from Donegal, the golden poteen from the Irish hills, silken poplin from Dublin, and honey from the heather fields—all these

9

were being loaded on board ship for sale in the globe of the world. And somewhere down the quays the fishing men were dragging their nets on board singing their chantey of "Herring, the King." *Pad-pad-pad* of the little donkeys of the hills, chattering of sea-gulls, creak of pulleys. Somewhere an old man playing a fiddle, and the *clank-clank* as an anchor was hove short. All about him was the shower of vital sunshine, except for the cool shadow when a cloud sailed below the sun. But the bustle and sunshine and the mewing of the gulls were nothing to Raftery, for his heart was heavy.

He had chosen a lonely part of the quay because of the great pulling on his heart, and he had no fancy to be talking to children or the idlers of the town. A queer figure he seemed there, so virile, so brooding, his great shoulders and bronzed face and hair riddled with grey, although as yet he had not come to forty years. His face was not like the faces of most blind men, pathetically open, child-like, and resigned, but was bitten by furrows, harsh even. His hands were muscular and beautiful. His eyes were shrouded by the lids like the eyes of a hawk. The only thing pathetic about him were his clothes, the neat brogues that were not properly cleaned, the knee-breeches with the garters not properly fastened, the fine linen with the wine-splotch on the bosom, and the velvet coat from which some silver buttons were missing, for from his face one could see how such little things would irk him. But Raftery's servant was an old soldier, and averse to work as old soldiers are, and a little inclined to be silently contemptuous toward the blind poet.

"Now that summer is coming," the blind man was saying to himself. His fingers were plucking idly at an end of rope he had picked up. His eyes were closed; his forehead taut with concentration.

"Now that summer is coming . . .

"Now that summer is coming," his voice spoke out in a low vibration,

"I will cut a blackthorn stick for my hand,
  And I will quit this loud town for the silence of the county of Mayo.
  And in that lake-dotted, heather-scented land,
  This old pain will go."

He was so intent that he did not hear the light footfall coming toward him delicately over the flagstones of the quay. . . . He leaned forward, his hands clasped.

"The rustle of rowan-trees and the wind among the
    rushes,
The otter plunging, the trout jumping in some high
    mountain lake,
The blackbird's fluting I must hear, and the sweet-
    throated thrushes,
Or my heart break."

The footfall ceased. She was standing still listening. He rose and threw out his hands.

"For I am sick of the talk of the wine-shop, and the talk
    of the merchant people;
The chatter of buying and selling and of how bad times
    are;
And of monks who whine for doles to build some grey
    church steeple,
And see no star."

Some little movement of hers, some involuntary rustle, must have struck his sensitive ear, for he stopped and turned uncannily toward her. He waited for her to speak.

"What song is that at you, dark man?" she asked him. Her voice was trembling. He puzzled for a moment over the quaint accent she put on the Erse words.

"It is a song," he said, "woman of Spain, of how sick my whole heart is of this crapulous

trading town, and of the great dignified con-
versations one can hold with high mountains,
and of the coldness and the cleanness of lake
water, and of the melodies birds sing in the
twilight and at the breaking of the day."

"Is there all this peace and healing then in
the County Mayo, blind poet?"

"There is, woman of Spain."

"You know me, then?" Her voice trembled
with a little of fear.

"I know you are of Spain by your accent,
and I know you are a small woman by the
point from which your voice comes. By your
voice, too, I know you are a lady. But who
you are, whether or not you are comely, and
what name is on you, I do not know."

"I am a woman of Spain, and I am not
uncomely, Raftery, and the name I have is
Hilaria."

"Hilaria means merry," Raftery pondered.
"It is a strange name for a sweet grave voice."

"Are you leaving this town now, Raftery?
Are you leaving it now for the county of
Mayo?"

"I am leaving it now, woman of Spain," he
answered her. "I am leaving it now as soon
as I can collect my few things and pay my
reckoning, for all my songs are sung, and

though the people are not tired of them, yet I am, and no new songs come in a market-place. By the sea-shore and the mountains and the little mountain lakes the songs are, shy as shy birds."

She was close to him now. He had an impression she was standing just below him, her face turned up to him like a flower on its stalk. He was vibrating within like one of the strings of his own harp, like one of the blue bass strings of his own harp.

"Do you go alone, blind Raftery, into the county of Mayo?"

"I go alone, woman of Spain, but for my servant and a packhorse."

"Have you no wife, then, Raftery?"

"I am no poor blind man to sit by a fire while a woman cooks. Though my eyes are empty, woman of Spain, I am an eagle in my ways."

"Nor any woman—woman to follow you?"

"There is no streeling woman to walk the roads and boast in wine-shops she is Raftery's darling."

"Nor brothers, nor home, Raftery?"

"Our home is gone. The trading men of Dublin tricked it from our people, and one of my brothers is a cornet with King Louis of

France and the other is a monk in Portugal. And I am a blind singer of the Connaught hills. But who are you, woman of Spain, to ask me these questions?"

"Are you crossing the street, blind Raftery? There is traffic on the street, and I am staying at your inn. Will you rest your elbow against my shoulder, blind Raftery?" She evaded his question.

"From whose house do you come?" he insisted.

"I come," she hesitated, "from—from Dafydd Evan's house."

"The Welshman of Claregalway's," he frowned. "The Welshman of Claregalway is no friend of mine."

"But the shoulder I offer you is not the Welshman of Claregalway's, blind Raftery. It is my own shoulder. May I not offer you that, dark man?"

"I am only a poor singer, but I am, I hope, an Irish gentleman," said Raftery. "For why should I hurt you, young woman of Spain?"

They crossed the bustling quay together, the big proud-faced blind poet and the little woman of Spain—her lustrous high-piled hair with the great comb in it, the dusky soft face, the brocade bodice like a breastplate, the belling skirt, the stockings of white silk and the shoes with high red heels, and the shawl of patterned green, the immense shawl of silk with the weight of a feather, and the big fan hanging from one wrist by its thong of soft red leather. She was a small slight woman, but about her was a great dignity. And when she raised her face to look at him, there was about it the exquisite quality of a golden mask. The lashes of the eyes were as though painted by a brush, and the brows were groomed into a high black curve, like oiled silk; against the gold of her face her mouth of old rose colour showed in a delicate tint. Her small soft nose, and her throat like a column of ivory, like warm new ivory.

They trod their way through the people of the quays, the tall mountainy people who took short quick steps, moving lightly as cats, the sailors rolling as to a heaving deck, the townspeople with their long hurried stride. The little brown donkeys pulled up for them, and the black shaggy ponies of the hills, and the great rough horses the countrymen rode. Delicately they made their way to the door of the inn.

"I thank you, young girl of Spain," Raftery said, "for your kindness and your shoulder."

"I thank you, Raftery," she said, "I thank you for letting me know you, blind man, from my heart and soul."

And she was up the stairs with a clicking of little heels. The landlord came out of the wine-room with a fine flourish.

"Let you come in here, Patrick Raftery, my fine poet, let you come in here. There is new sand on the floor here and a piper of Achill Island, and a great new drink I have thought up for you, champagne wine of France, and brandy of France, and they mixed together."

"'Tis I will need it," said Raftery, "for there is a shadow between me and the sun."

"Is it the want of money, Patrick Raftery? Is it short you'd think we'd let you be?"

"It is not, man of the house, and thank you kindly!"

"Is it that anyone's been making little of you, singing lad? If so he's a dead man before this night is out. There's no lack of knives in Galway City."

"No, no, man of the house."

"Is it the want of your eyes has come on you suddenly, my poor dark fellow?"

"It is the Welshman of Claregalway," Raftery said, "has come between me and the sun."

17

CHAPTER III

In no country of the world has there been such mixture of races as Ireland has seen. Out of Africa had come the black men of Par-Thelon and abode there until the sickness of the lungs had blotted them from the face of the green land. And the ancient Britons had come, King Arthur's peons, the short squat men who dug underground as in Wales and Cornwall for tin and gold and coal. The Firbolgs, the men with the bags, we call them in our scant guerrilla history. After them followed the people of Dana, whose origin and whose history and whose end no man knows. And for many centuries there hovered over Ireland seven sinister veils of magic, so that even great Cæsar would not attempt its conquest. The hardy red Danes swept Ireland, so Dublin became a Danish city, and all there is left of their invasion are the names of the places: Leixlip, and Wexford, and Waterford, and the story of the lost formula of the heather ale, and the heads of red golden hair the women have that put shame on the Venetian ladies, so rich, so wonderful that colour is.

And after them came the Normans, that race which nothing could kill, huge men on huge horses, with mace and battleaxe, and they abode there, becoming more Irish than the Irish, *ipses*, say historians, *ipses hiberniis hiberniores*. And against them came from the North of Scotland the raiding Highland clans, under Edward de Bruce, great Robert's brother. Great claymores swung by their sides, in their deep leather belts were thrust short battleaxes, and there were short keen knives in stockings and under their armpits. The tune their pipes skirled was " Cogadh No Sith!"

> . . . cuma linn, is cuma linn cogadh no sith
> Marbhamor sa cogadh, no crochamar san sith!
> It's all the same to us whether it's war or peace.
> For in war we are killed, and in peace they hang us.

Great magnificent ruffians those—their strain and tongue remain in the highlands of Ulster, and Edward de Bruce, king of Ireland, is buried there, as a pledge, so old men say. In Foughart graveyard he is buried standing, sword in hand, on watch by the marches of

Ulster, his keen hawk's face turned southward. . . .

Out of England came mincing Essex, came great Cromwell the lord protector, came Dutch William the king and Duke Schomberg, and each left behind him the trace of their blood and hand. But came now a newer invasion, against whom arms were no defence and fighting no glory or pleasure. Came trading men who fought the careless, dicing, fighting, hunting Irish nobles with the weapon of credit. Did any one need money? There was money for them. A hunting horse? A racing boat? They produced everything, like a jinnee of Arabian myth. And suddenly one day some greasy scullion arrived with a writ, and one by one the old families faded away, some to France to die with Patrick Sarsfield at Fontenoy, some to High Germany to seek service with the prince palatine or the emperor, some to Spain, some to Portugal, some to the American Carolinas. More of the Wild Geese spread wing to rid themselves of the parasites of commerce than ever sailed with Patrick Sarsfield from Limerick Quay.

They were all over the shattered country now, buying up debts, taking up and foreclosing mortgages, lending money at ruinous rates, assisting the great families to ruin. And when the families had gone, they came in, occupying the big noble houses and the fair lands. And chief of them in Connaught was Dafydd Evans, who was known to the country-side as the Welshman of Claregalway.

Only once had Raftery met him, but the memory of that meeting remained with him and the country-side and the Welshman for years. Raftery was returning from a tour of Munster, where he had visited all the great houses, singing, composing, harping at each of them. And on his way back through Connaught he had heard tales of Evans wherever he went. Of this demesne bought up, of these jewels in pawn to the Welshman, of the Lynchs of Ballylynch crossing the sea to the wild colony of Maryland. No pestilence or war could have cleared the country of these families, but the grasping fingers of the grabbers did. And of them the greatest was Dafydd Evans of Claregalway.

He had been coming up the long Connaught road, grey of winter twilight in the air, striding forward holding the great Irish wolf-hound who guided him on a short leash. Behind him walked his servant leading the Iceland pony on which the harp was packed.

"There is a great house on the hill, please your Honour," said the old soldier. He wore the faded blue and red uniform in which he had fought in the Low Countries, the high grenadier's cap. "There is a great glow from the windows."

"What townland are we now in?"

"We are in the townland of Claregalway, please your Honour!"

"Then 'tis the Welshman's house?"

"Would it please your Honour to go up there?" asked the old soldier. "There would be warm fires there and mulled wine, and feather-beds, please your Honour, in painted rooms."

"It would very much hurt my honour," said blind Raftery. "We will go to a public inn."

And he strode forward, the wolf-dog padding beside him, while the old soldier brought up the pony grumbling, as old soldiers will.

There was welcome and cheer at the village inn. By some obscure telepathy it became known that Raftery was lying there the night, and from little cottages in the bogs and little houses in the hillsides the countrymen came in frieze-coats, and the women came in long blue cloaks to set eyes on Raftery. A still night it was, frost making a little skim of ice

22

on the black bog waters, and a hazy mist rising in the air, and in the air a great honey-coloured moon up. From far and wide they came, silent, respectful. The man of the inn tapped his best liquors, brown Scottish ale and the dark Irish stout, and the golden peat-scented whisky of the hills, and brandy that had been smuggled from France, and claret that had the bite of young grapes in it, and Italian wines in bottles cunningly covered with straw. And those who had money could pay for it, and those who had not might drink anyway, for great Raftery was in the house. And Raftery himself, smiling, brought his harp and played for them, not the deep heart-searching songs he himself had written, but the lays of the country-side, like "The Palatine's Daughter," and "Brady's Lament."

O List to the plaint of a poor Irish harper,
    And scorn not the strains from his aged withered hand.
Remember his fingers could once move more sharper,
    To rise up the glories of his dear native land.
When I was young King James he did flourish,
    And I followed the wars in my brogues bound with straw,
And all the pretty colleens from Wexford to Durrish
    Called me the bold Phelim Brady, the Bard of Armagh.

He could hear the quiet chuckles of delight from his country audience as he told the loved tune on the plunking harp-strings. He swept suddenly into the soft minor with the bass like the drone of a pipe, of a pipe playing some passionate lament.

When Mother Death in her soft arms will embrace me,
    Low lull me to sleep with sweet "Erin Go Bragh,"
By the side of my Kathleen, my young wife, oh, place me,
    And forget Phelim Brady, the Bard of Armagh.

His hands fell from the strings, and he felt the silence of the audience which is the real applause, then a little volley of hand-clappings, a chatter in Erse, which stopped suddenly, as someone came into the pleasant sanded tap-room. The entry came to Raftery as of some cold and moist thing, some strange inhuman thing, as of the sea. He stood up resting his hand on the keyboard.

"What manner of man," Raftery asked, "has come into this room?"

"It is Dafydd Evans has come into this room, Master Raftery," came the soft sibilant Welsh voice. "Dafydd Evans of Claregalway."

So often had he been described to him that Raftery could evoke his appearance on the screen of his sensitive grey brain. The funereal black clothes, the abject attitude, the huge face with the melancholy hypocritical eyes, the high bald forehead, the jowl flabby as a blood-hound's, the scraggy neck, the small pendulous belly, the thin shanks, the fat moist hands.

"I am not Master Raftery," Raftery said coldly. "I am Patrick Raftery, Esquire, of Abbeyraftery."

"I know your quality, Patrick Raftery," went the Welshman's buttery tones, "and for that reason I have come to invite you to my big house away from this boozing den. For I love the harp and the timbrel and chief musicians. I have a fine house, yea, pleasant."

"I do not doubt it, Welshman," said Raftery dryly.

"And I would reward you, Raftery. I would give you gold, yea, fine gold."

But Raftery said nothing. He sat down by his harp, fingering the bass softly.

"And you would make a song about me, Raftery, that would be remembered. A song such as you make about the Irish kings and the Irish families, Raftery. A song or psalm, great Raftery," he pleaded.

"A song on you, such as will be remembered, Welshman," Raftery laughed. "A song such as I make of Irish kings and Irish families. Yes, I will make a song about you, Welshman."

The fingers crashed into the harp-strings.

"Crowns of glory in high heaven," he sang, "for King
    Rory and King Brian.
Suits of armour for Fitz-Simon and O'Rourke and
    O'Ryan,
But in hell the proud devils, well they wouldn't waste
    the fire
For Dafydd Evans of Llanelly in Glamorganshire!"

The Welshman turned silently and went
out of the door. For one instant there was
silence, then ringing laughter, and the rapid
chatter of Erse. Yes, the quatrain would be
remembered. The man of the inn stood by
Raftery.

"He will never forgive you, Raftery."

"Why?" laughed Raftery.

"You have hurt his pride."

"Have these people pride as well as riches?
Feelings as well as grasping hands?" Raftery
asked.

"He will do some hurt, Raftery."

"He cannot. I have no money to be
taken away from me. O man of the inn,
call up that young piper and bid my soldier
get his flute, for we will play music for dancing. There is one sound that raises my
heart. It is the feet of young women softly
dancing."

CHAPTER IV

THERE is about this town of Galway a strange benign glamour. Moss grows upon the ancient quays, and there is a soft hush in the air, and the sea does glamourous magic. "The City of the Tribes" it is called, though why men can only surmise. Grey with the soft greyness of old people who have achieved rest, sunny with a sun that is like golden wine in nerve and blood, and sometimes a vast purple shadow comes over it and it is like a city one might see in a dream, so peaceful, so dreaming, so pleasantly old. It was from the town of Galway that Blessed Brendan sailed westward on a summer eve, and it was from Galway that Columbus' shrewd navigator came, so I have heard it claimed and no man gainsay it. And it is from the cliffs of Galway that one sees Hy Brasil, the island that is beautiful as its name, and there is great argument as to whether Hy Brasil is a seeming of old Atlantis thrown by sun magic from the ocean bed to the screen of the high white clouds, or whether it is in reality Tir nan Og, the Gaelic heaven. Myself, I do not know.

But I would have nobody think that Galway was always a peaceful city, for there is no credit to that. Many's the gallant fight she has seen against the raiding Moors of Barbary, great burly men, who leaped ashore waving their weapons and declaring there is no God but God. Great sincere fighters, but they got their bellyful on Galway quay. The proud ghost of their gallantry remains in the soft Atlantic air. . . . When one is crushed and heartbroken, it is good to travel to Galway Town.

Right between you and far America there is nothing but salt deep water, where roam the salmon and the porpoise and Herring the King. There is only the green Atlantic meadows until you come to Alpin Nua, New Scotland, or Nova Scotia as some pedant has named it on the maps, or if you go southward until you come to the dainty coralline Bermudas. At evening the sun lingers over this last of old Europe, and there is a twilight longer than any twilight in the world, blue overhead and reddish golden on the horizon, so that you wonder if you have not died in some gentle afternoon sleep and are wandering now on the edge of the promised peaceful country, where the boughs of the trees are golden and silver, gold blossoms on silver branches, and the fights are all merry unbitter ones, and there is honey and ale for all.

The door of the wine-shop had opened, and Raftery was coming up the short steps to the street in the dusk. The throaty murmur of a little song came to him, and the thrumming of a guitar, the soft nostalgic thrumming of some deep-toned guitar. A little height above the street was the balcony of the principal guest-room of the inn, a room of high windows of the Latin kind, that opened on to a balcony as doors open.

"Is that you who are playing, woman of Spain?"

"Yes," came the answer, "yes, Raftery."

"It is not a merry song, woman of Spain."

"It is a song of some of the women of Cadiz, Raftery. A song of the women who are merry because they are paid to be merry, and love because it is their trade to love, and this is what it says, in the Irish tongue. 'Hush, heart, hush. The day is gone by at last, and to-morrow—who knows?—you may be happy, for God remembers—remembers even us.'"

"That **is** a sad song to be singing, girl called Hilaria."

He reached out and rested his hand on the

iron uprights of the balcony. His brown fingers were within a few inches of her velvet-covered foot.

"It is the first song come to my lips, Raftery. So soft has the summer day been and so gentle is the twilight, and here the sea goes westward as it goes westward from the town of Cadiz, that my heart moved within me, and I took up this instrument and sang a song, Raftery. It is a sad song," she insisted, "but it does not mean that I am sad."

"Are you lonely for Cadiz, woman of Spain?"

"I am not, Raftery. For here is the soft and yet harsh land that Spain is, and here is romance, and here a gentle twilight, and the gigantic Atlantic sea. And all I miss are the girls of Cadiz, and their bright shawls, and the men singing songs to the women at the close of day."

"The women of Ireland are not gay, Hilaria. When evening comes they are on their knees praying for forgiveness of their sins, though what sins these are God only knows. But so they are taught, Hilaria, that the evenings are not for laughter and love-making and soft human things, but to pray in. It is an evil doctrine and a sin itself, I'm thinking, but as for singing songs"—he smiled—"am I not here?"

"O Raftery," her voice came eager and swift, "to-night in the dusk you look young. This morning you seemed bitter, and old for your years, Raftery, but to-night you seem young."

"It is usual for me to be bitter and old," he said, "for if I had my eyes I would be carving out my fortune in the foreign wars, and not be a wandering poet of Connaught. It is a hard thing, Hilaria, to have the heart of a fighting man, and blind eyes. But sometimes I am happy, as to-night. Shall I make a song for you, and for the sake of this city, Hilaria, that you will not be missing too much the men singing under the windows of Cadiz?"

"But you do not know me, Raftery; how could you make a song for me? You have never seen me, not that I am so much worth seeing," she said.

"Below in the wine-shop," he told her, "there is no talk but of your beauty. They have left the talk of fighting and the talk of sport to the talking of your comeliness and grace."

"O Raftery, no!" There was a catch in her breath. "What do they say?" she asked fearfully.

"They're saying it's true," he sang softly, "that your
    shoe is the smallest yet seen.
And a man from the south says your mouth is the
    mouth of a queen.

The boatmen of the cape claim your shape is like the
  wild swan's on the wind—
They retail me all this, lest I miss so much wonder,
  being blind."

"But, Raftery, I am not beautiful. I am
only young and a little pretty. And if my
shoe is small it is because I am a small woman
O Raftery, they are telling you what is not
true."

"I know it myself, Hilaria. When you
came to the quay this morning there blew
toward me a current of beauty and youth that
I shook from head to foot. Listen, Hilaria:

"By Corrib's long lake there shake the broad chestnut-
  trees;
Every blossom and rod must nod to the soft moorland
  breeze—
So trembled my whole heart and soul when I leaned on
  your arm,
And you crossed the wide street on swift feet to guide
  me past harm."

"O Raftery, you are only singing that.
You are only singing a song. These feelings
could not have come to you, Raftery. O
Raftery, it is a shame to sing such songs."

"O woman of Spain," he went on, "the pain you have
  put in my heart,
To tell you its tenth would surpass the strength of my
  art.

There is on me a grief past belief, and no man in this
    place,
But pities my plight without sight of your fair Latin
    face."

"You are only singing a song, Raftery. I
know you. You are doing it to make me feel
less lonely. You are singing as you imagine
the men singing to the girls of Cadiz."

"And if I weren't, woman of Spain, if I were
singing out of my heart——"

"If you were singing out of your heart—"
her voice caught. "Ah, but you aren't,
Raftery. You are paying me compliments.
And they are great compliments, for I can see
the pride on an Irishwoman's face if she could
say, 'Great Raftery once made a poem about
my beauty,' and how that would set her above
the people of her day."

"If we were below," he sang, "in Mayo, where the tall
    rowan stands;
In the County Kildare, or in Clare of the wide golden
    sands,
The hours would pass by as fly the swift swallows of
    spring,
While you listened with pride by my side to the poems
    I would sing."

"Where is your hand, Raftery," she asked.
"I cannot see, now it is dark. Ah, I have it,"
she leaned over the balcony. "I must stay

out here no longer, Raftery, and in all I know I have no words to thank you. You sang a song to me as you thought the men sing to the girls of Cadiz, and it was a light thing in your mind for all you say, but your song, Raftery, it is written deep in my heart."

"My song was a poor thing, woman of Spain," Raftery answered, "but a light thing it was not. And the hand you gave me, I shall never forget, for though I cannot see, I can feel. I can feel its small fingers softly on my heart." He kissed it and raised his face to her.

"The summer rain is coming"—he felt two warm drops on his face. "You must go within, woman of Spain."

She laughed a little. "Yes, the rain is coming," she said, "and I must go in. Good night, and thank you, Patrick Raftery."

"Good night, woman of Spain."

"Patrick Raftery, go with God!"

He went down the steps to the wine-shop, when she had closed the windows. The burly innkeeper greeted him with boisterous affection.

"Let me get a drink for you, Patrick Raftery, to keep out the afflictions on the night air." He waddled behind his counter. "Sure I was bothered stiff with the fear of you catching cold out there, and you courting and cajoling the woman of Spain."

"Will you mind your own business, man of the house!"

"Now, what matter, Patrick Raftery! But why did you come in so sudden?"

"There is rain coming," Raftery said. "I could feel the warm drops on my face."

"'Tis a pity so," said the landlord, "that the courting must stop, for 'tis niece she is, I hear, to the Welshman of Claregalway, and he'll be here by the dawn of day.

"''Twill be queer so," the landlord rambled on, "to have the pair of you in the one house, him that has the power of money, and you that have the power of verse, and that made his name a laughing-stock the country over by saying the devils would think so little of him as to begrudge him the coals of hell——"

"''Twas a great mistake you made, Patrick Raftery"—the Aran pot-boy had gone out to look at the night, and had now come in—"and you thinking there was rain in it, and the warm drops on your face, for the stars are standing up in the sky," he said, "and there is not a cloud the size of a silver sixpence in art or part of the high air."

CHAPTER V

THE old soldier servant had shaved him, his hand shaking rather badly from potations on the quays the night before, and was helping him into his velvet coat, when a knocking came to the door.

"Will you see who that is, sergeant?"

"It is a man, and he wishing to talk to you, please your Honour."

"He would do well to wait until later in the day, when my humour is better," grumbled Raftery. "What man is in it, so?"

"It is the Welshman of Claregalway, please, your Honour."

"Ha, Welshman!" He turned round to face the door. "What is it you have to say to Raftery?"

"I come in friendship, Patrick Raftery," the singsong oily Welsh tones went, "no enmity, whatever. No, indeed. Is this the way you greet friends, Raftery *bach*, dear Raftery?"

"It is not the way I greet friends, Welshman. There is no covenant of friendship between me and you. Are you come," he sneered, "to have me make another verse about you?"

"I have come," said the Welshman, after a little pause, "I have come about my ward, Hilaria.

"Come with me, Raftery; I have a little withdrawing-room in the hotel. And if you wish wine, we will have it, for there is nothing I would grudge, Raftery, to show my friendship to you."

"I wish no wine, Welshman, but lead the way, and your shoulder, sergeant." They passed along the corridors and entered a little room. "Open the windows, sergeant, that the sun may come. Open the windows and go. And now, Welshman."

"Your voice is harsh, Raftery." The oily tones went on. "Maybe you think I bear you enmity for the verse you wrote against me, and that they sing over the countryside. No enmity, whatever," he purred. "You do not know me, Raftery *bach*."

Raftery edged his chair further away. Though he could not see Evans, yet before his mind there rose up the picture of the man, like some obscene creature of the woods. The black clothes, the belly in the lap of the thin legs, the neck ugly as ewe's, the bald high forehead, the eyes black and small and shiny as marbles, the ungainly nose all cartilage and skin, the sucking purple lips, the dewlap like a hound's. There came from him a cold moistness, as from some clammy misshapen ghost, that was repellent to the strength and health of Raftery.

"Well, what of—Hilaria?"

"You know Hilaria. You have seen Hilaria, Raftery——"

"I cannot see."

"But you have leaned on her shoulder, Raftery. You know how warm and soft her shoulder is. You have talked to her, Raftery. You know her voice is like honey. It is rich as golden honey. You talked to her last evening, Raftery." He leaned over and touched the poet on the knee. "Raftery, the marrying time for Hilaria is come."

Raftery thought for an instant. His right hand slid to his left armpit.

"I may be a blind man," he said quietly, "but you are a dead one, if those words are not taken back." And he flicked the heavy razor-edged knife out of its scabbard. The Welshman rose with a squeal of terror.

"Oh, I did not mean that, Raftery," he whined. "I did not mean that. You are the vessel of honour, Patrick Raftery. And my ward is a modest woman, chaste, exceedingly chaste. But I would give her to you in marriage, Patrick Raftery, if you would have her, and she is a woman in a thousand, yea, ten thousand!"

Raftery said nothing.

"You need a wife, Raftery. See your fine velvet coat, how the silver buttons are missing, and your hose that need mending, and your money that needs taking care of. And oh, the pleasantness of having a fine wife, Raftery, no more loneliness in the evenings or nights, and she is pleasant all over, like her shoulder, Raftery, like her honey voice——"

"Why give her to me? I am only a poor blind poet."

"You are poor and blind, Raftery, but who gets what honours you receive? There is no house in the Irish nation where you are not an honoured guest, houses where I would be ranked with the scullions. And the peasants would give you money for nothing, when to me they would not pay their debts. You are a great man, Raftery."

"Is your niece Hilaria rich?"

"Alas, no, she is not rich, Raftery. She is not my niece; she is my ward. There was a merchant of Spain, oh! a good man, Raftery, but not foreseeing; and when he died he left nothing and I took her and reared her out of kindness, yea, charity. And she has cost me money, Raftery, much money. But I will give money with her, Raftery, not too much money, for I am not so rich as people say——"

"I want no money," said Raftery.

"Then you will marry her, Raftery. You can marry her this morning. The Shepelaun More is a good friend to me, and he will marry you. He is a good friend, the Shepelaun More."

The Shepelaun More, or Big Chaplain, was the head cleric of Galway Town. A great florid man who had been a captain-at-arms in the Low Countries, and had become cleric, he made no disguise about it, because preaching was better for the pocket than blows. A burly venal man was the Shepelaun More.

"What does Hilaria say of all this?"

"She is willing, yea, eager, Raftery. She is a strange woman. I shall send for her."

He went outside and called a servant. "She would rather have the open road than a house, and rather be free than rich, Raftery. For all her comeliness, she is hard to tire, Raftery. It is good business, your marrying Hilaria.

"And I give Hilaria to you, Raftery, to show that I am a good man, yea, godly. For you wrote a harsh poem about me, that the country people sing to my face. For I do good to them that hurt me, Patrick Raftery."

"The more damned fool you!" the poet laughed.

A cold and bitter blast of enmity seemed to strike the back of Raftery's neck. There was hatred in the room, black writhing hatred. It accorded ill with the Welshman's oily words.

"But here is Hilaria!"

Raftery rose, turned his bronzed face to the door. He heard the minute tap of her little feet upon the floor. There came to his nostrils the faint breath of roses.

"The Welshman says you will marry me, woman of Spain."

"If you will have me, Patrick Raftery."

"Indeed I will have you, woman of Spain. But I cannot see why you should marry me, for 'tis a poor bargain you're getting."

"There are three reasons why I should marry you, Patrick Raftery. The one is that already I love you, and a second is that you need me, and the third, if it suits you, I will keep to myself.

"O Raftery," she came close to him, and her voice trembled, as though she were on the point of tears, "believe me, there is no man will ever have a truer, more patient, more loyal wife than I will be to you, Patrick Raftery."

"But I am only a poor poet, Hilaria. There are peddling chapmen who have more than I, for all my entry into great houses. And if the poetry were to go from me, Hilaria, what should I do? I am only a poor Irish gentleman and would not accept charity. What should we do then, Hilaria, but starve?"

"While I have ten fingers to work, and two eyes to see, you shall never starve. But there are three conditions I make before I marry you."

"And they, Hilaria?"

"The first is, when you are tired of me, or have cause for anger against me, that you put me away."

Raftery laughed. Like the laughter of some

thin mean ghost came the sniggering of the Welshman.

"And the second is, Raftery, when we are travelling from town to town, if there is only food for one, that I go without; if in an inn there is only room for one, that I am the one to remain without. Promise me this, Patrick Raftery."

"There is no need for this, Hilaria. Our country is a poor country, but not so poor that the wife or a friend of Patrick Raftery need lack a meal or a roof for the night. And your other condition," he smiled, "small, grave Hilaria?"

"O Raftery," she pleaded, "let me not make that until we are married and on our road to the county of Mayo. It is not a great condition, nor one that you will think hard to refuse, dear Raftery. But may I keep it, please, until we are on the road, and away from this town, and the many people? Please, dear Raftery."

"There is no condition I would refuse to you, small dark Hilaria."

"You are a lucky man, Raftery," the oily voice of the Welshman broke in. "It is written, 'Who can find a virtuous woman? for her price is far above rubies.' And I found you a woman, Raftery, though you wrote harsh verse about me. Your heart can safely trust in her, Raftery *bach*——"

The door opened, and Evans's thin, precise servant entered.

"They are ready at the church, sir. The witnesses are ready, and the Shepelaun More."

"Whom did you find for witnesses?" Evans drew the man aside.

"A drunken grave-digger," the servant grinned, "and a woman of the town."

"Good, good." The Welshman's loose wabbly lips went into a moist wide smile. "It is good, yea, excellent! O Raftery," he called aloud, "your wedding is ready, great poet, whom lords love to honour. O Raftery, your wedding is ready."

CHAPTER VI

IT seemed to Raftery that on going into the great grey church they were leaving the world and going into some deep, unpleasant hiding-place. Outside was sunshine and the singing of the birds, fat blackbird and thrush and thieving wood-pigeon, and the meadow-lark whose wings are never quiet and whose song is like the ringing of the distant fairy bells. Into the grey church light came subdued and secret; the golden sunshine was annulled by panes stained purple and yellow and blue. An artificer's hand barred out the golden vital sun, and of birds' sweet melodies there were none, nor any voice of them at all, barring the hoarse harshness of the rook. Though he could not see, yet everywhere he could feel secrecy, privacy. Lamps lighted in the middle of God's day. No life, but a dankness as of a latrine. A queer place to meet God in, Raftery thought. Was it not more likely they would find Him, if they really wanted

Him, in the quiet of Achill Island at the close of day, when the small waves slapped the beach of little singing pebbles. and the little wind of sundown rustled the grasses and the trees; or in the morning striding the great purple Connemara peaks, or by some cool mountain well surrounded by soft russet moss, in a green nook of the mountains where the plover fussed in the heather about her little nest? Anywhere there they might come on Him. But this secret left-handed house, surely this was no place to meet a Gentleman, thought blind Raftery.

Their footsteps made a ringing hollow sound as they walked up the nave, a deep uncomely sound as though walking in a great tomb. Even Hilaria, her small light feet made a low leaden sound.

"Is all well with you, small Hilaria?"

"Soon all will be well with me, Patrick Raftery."

They came to where a loud purring voice accosted them.

"So this is Raftery, the great Raftery?" And Raftery knew he was standing before the Shepelaun More. His hand was grasped by a fat moist hand. He fixed his mind on a picture of the Shepelaun More. Once a young Sligo poet had described him for Raftery, a huge frame of a man, with a great jaw and good teeth, a hooked nose and fine broad brow and a fringe of white reverend hair like a halo.

"That is a good face for a man," Raftery had said.

"But he has woman's eyes," the Sligo man had added, "sly, subtle eyes."

And now under the florid mask Raftery could imagine the small green treacherous eyes; behind the purr of the voice he could sense the selfishness of the cat, the cat's sharp claws.

"I like your poems, great Raftery," the Shepelaun More complimented him. "'The Green Woods of Truagh' is ever on my lips, and that beautiful, that exquisite thing about the queen of Scots. 'Her hands are long and dagger-shaped——'" he began to quote.

"Yes, they are good poems," said Raftery brusquely.

"Yes, but you have made mean poems, too," said the Shepelaun More reprovingly. "You made a poem about our brother and good friend here, Dafydd Evans, a poem against him. It was not generous of you, Patrick Raftery."

"I did not come into this cold place,"
Raftery said, "to discuss either my poems or
the virtues of the Welshman of Claregalway.
I came here to be married, and I have brought
a ring for the wedding, and ten golden guineas
for you, chaplain, to put in your pouch. So
go ahead and marry me."

"I will marry you, Raftery." The chap-
lain's voice was cold and edged with hatred.
"I will marry you to this woman so tightly
that not all the bishops in this land, nor God
Himself, no! nor even the Holy Father at
Rome, could break this marriage."

"Do so, then."

"Kneel down, both of you," said the
Shepelaun More.

She took his elbow and guided him, and
knelt beside him, so close that he could feel her
praying. Within her something in a long blue
garment was crying aloud to God, was seeking
to pierce through this harsh stone house and
go upward to God. For all her dignity and
beauty, beside him he felt her to be some small
dark child who was bothered and clouded, and
naked with sincerity. Above him the big
vestmented man was reading the Latin service
with a cynical, ribald intonation as though he
were celebrating some blasphemy of black

diabolist rites instead of a sanctity of God. The strange sincere child beside him and the ribald priest above him. Raftery began to mutter.

"What is it, Raftery?" said the Shepelaun More, with his soft Southern insincere voice.

"I beg your pardon, chaplain. I beg of you a thousand pardons," Raftery said humbly. "My mind was rambling, Shepelaun More, and I was at the making of a poem——"

"An epithalamium? Some delicate fancy for a poet's wedding, eh, Patrick Raftery?"

"'Twas this," said Raftery, and his voice rang through the church like a trumpet.

"O cleric with a harlot's face,
  Sprung from the race of Kerrymen—"

"Raftery," the Shepelaun More interrupted savagely, "will you have this woman for your wedded wife?"

"I will."

"Say: 'I, Patrick, take thee, Hilaria——'"

"I, Patrick, take thee, Hilaria——"

And so the service went ahead with its sonority of Latin beating against grey wall and grey statue, gaudy painting and gaudy window.

Without, the God of the Gael went about his business, tending his birds and bees, and flinging great drifts of hawthorn over the green hillsides, and striding the slopes of the mountains, where graze the white silent sheep, walking the curling waters where the herring show silver in the sun, watching the lordly salmon fling himself high over the Shannon's weirs, or resting by some oak-tree, a tall young god with great wheaten beard, who had small time for the prudish rite of marriage in churches. So out of a grey past the Shepelaun More invoked a harsh alien god, an aged cursing god to bless the marriage of the Irish poet and the Spanish lady. . . .

The Shepelaun More closed his book with a slap.

"Now you are married, Patrick Raftery. Here is your wedded wife. Here is Dafydd Evans, who gave the bride away. Here am I. Here are your witnesses."

"What work is at you, honest man?" asked Raftery.

"I do be digging graves."

"'Tis a mournful work, honest man."

"Some one must put the poor dead in their beds. Who are more helpless than poor dead people?"

"Ay, so they are," Raftery thought. "And you, good woman, what name is on you?"

"A bad name," she whispered.

"I have known a bad name," said Raftery, "go with a warm heart."

"My heart is warm to nothing, Patrick Raftery, but poor shivering children and over-laden donkeys and beaten dogs."

"Is not that enough?" said Raftery. He felt Hilaria's small fingers take his arm and press. "I thank you both for coming to help me. It was good of you." He put his hand in his pocket.

"Let you be giving me no money, Patrick Raftery," said the grave-digger, "for 'tis rich I am, with the thanks of the dead people and your own kindly words."

"I take no money from any man," said the woman, "that I do not earn. And I am in your debt, Patrick Raftery, for showing me what I seldom see—a very courteous gallant gentleman." And they walked down the long hollow aisle.

Raftery took a handful of gold-pieces from his pocket. "Take ten and give them to the cleric, Hilaria," he said. He heard the money jingle into the pocket of the Shepelaun More. "O chaplain, big or little, we are now quits."

A high cackle of laughter rose the echoes of the church. A tearing obscene sound, such as some ghostly bird might give by midnight in a cursed spot.

"And we are quits, too," the Welshman laughed. "You and I, Patrick Raftery. You made a poem about me. Go now into great houses with your poems. Bring your wife, too, and see what honour they give you, yea, what welcome. For the wife you have married——"

Raftery felt Hilaria leave his side in a quick leap. He heard the snick he recognised as a small dagger is drawn from a metal sheath. Evans's voice ceased, and hers came in a throbbing murmur.

"Before God, Dafydd Evans, one more word from you, and I shall not be the wife of Patrick Raftery, but the wife of the hangman and the gallows-tree."

"Come hither, Hilaria," Raftery ordered. He took the small weapon from her hand. "When there is any killing to be done, I, though blind, can do it; or my body-servant can, where it honour a man too much to be killed by me. Out of the way, Welshman," he thundered, "or I shall make a poem will rot the living flesh from your bones."

She led him from the high altar toward the door, outside which there were sunshine and bees droning.

"My Hilaria," he told her, "it was a poor wedding, and with poor people there, and I am afraid it is a poor husband you have, Hilaria."

"Raftery"—she laid her forehead for an instant on his arm—"let me not think what a husband I have, or humility will make my heart break. And as to the wedding, to-night when we journey north, and over the purple hills come to some white village, before we enter, Raftery, let me kneel in the twilight under some kindly tree, and take my heart out of my bosom, Raftery, and pray. And your hand will rest on my shoulder, and maybe you, too"—she looked up at him pleadingly—"will ask a blessing, Raftery, and we journeying northward into the county of Mayo."

CHAPTER VII

So they left Galway City on an afternoon
of May, with all the summer and the county
of Mayo before them. Behind them dropped
the brutish Norman buildings, the wide
squares, the Spanish-like houses, the banners
cracking in the salt breeze of Arran. Behind
them dropped the little thatched houses.
They passed the drinking-house of Jamaica
Jim, the great copper-coloured wrestler with
gold rings in his ears, who had broken the
back of the king of Portugal's bear. He was
playing a soft Carib song on a long flute with
great silver keys on it in the shade of his
sanded door-step. And there Sergeant Murphy stood still.

"Please your Honour," he called, "I go
no further on this road."

Raftery pulled the grey mare around.
"Come here," he said softly; "come close,"
he said, "until we talk this over." But the
sergeant would not budge.

"I will not go within reach of your hands, please your Honour"—the sergeant stood erect and dignified in his high grenadier hat and old blue coat with red facings—"for this is not a matter of petty mutiny or insubordination. I would follow your Honour to the end of the world."

"And why stop here then, sergeant?"

"There is now a lady in it, your Honour. And it is not punctilio, as the Spaniards say, for a military man to follow a woman, but, begging her ladyship's pardon, for a woman to follow a military man.

"And moreover, your Honour, in some town or village we come to, some cheap humorous citizen might make light of me, calling me skivvy or *feel de shomber*, as the French say, or other vile intolerable name, so that for the minor offence of striking a knife in his gizzard, they might make me dance the devil's hornpipe at the end of a greased rope. So that your Honours would be worse off if I left you that way than if I left you now."

"Hell to you," Raftery called furiously, "and your long words, and your tuppenny dignity! How am I to do without a body-servant?"

"This negro or coloured man, please your Honour," the sergeant explained, "is a great rogue and thief entirely, and he has always some man under lock and key to sell to the captains of ships, so that here you might get a better man than myself even, if it please your Honour."

"*A Shamus a Caha*, James of the Wrestling," Raftery called, "come here to me."

The big Carib shambled forward, his flute in his hand. He looked up suddenly.

"Before God," he cried, "it's Master Raftery."

"Have you anybody could tend me, wrestler, for the sergeant and I part here?"

"Master Raftery," the coloured man told him, "I have none here but a wild Highland boy with teeth like a trap, and a knife."

"Bring him out, then." He laid his hand on the mare's neck and slipped out of the saddle. "Come hither, boy," he called. "Come hither to me. I cannot see you. I am blind."

He put his hand out and caught the lad to him, ran his fingers over the boy's face, over the boy's shoulders and arms.

"I am Raftery," he said, "the principal poet of the Irish nation. Look at me. Do you like my face?"

"It is a good face," said the boy, simply.

"Look at this lady," Raftery directed. "Do you like her?"

"She is a very beautiful lady, and, I think, kind."

"Boy, would you like to follow us?"

"Sir," the boy answered, "I don't know much for a poet's service, but I can take care of your horse and your dog, and nothing will be stolen from you while you have me. I am a poor hand with a needle but good with a knife. I can tickle trout and snare game. Also I can steal fowl noiselessly, because," he said, "I was two years gillie to a Scottish laird in Argyle."

"Good!" said Raftery. "Hilaria, how does this boy seem?"

"He is tall, Raftery. Not so tall as you, but tall. He wears a grey frieze coat, and a yellow tunic and a yellow kilt, with a broad leather belt. And in the belt, Raftery"—she laughed—"is a knife like a butcher's cleaver. I have never seen so many freckles, Raftery, or such large red hands. But he has grey loyal eyes."

"Enough! Sergeant, unloose the great hound. Boy, go take him."

"He has walked up to the big wolf-dog," said Hilaria, "as if it were only a lap-dog. And with one hand he has taken its collar, and with the other he is rubbing its ears."

"He will do," said Raftery. "Wrestler, what money do you want for this servant-boy?"

"I would want no money, Raftery, but a favour of you, in your goings and comings."

"If it is drinking——" frowned Raftery.

"It is not that," said James of the Wrestling, "but that you, going up and down the counties and cities and villages of Ireland, will meet and hear talk of the bullies and fighting fellows. And if you hear any screeching with pride, would you tell him that for ten guineas he can have his fill of fighting and bloody murder at the hands of Shamus Crawford, the black man, at the sign of the Duck and Dragoon, in Galway City. No weight, holds, or style barred, and any worthy man without the money," he said, "can have a fight for the fun of it."

"I'll tell them, Shamus," Raftery said, "and now, sergeant, you're on your way."

"I'm on my way, please your Honour, to the lowlands of Holland, where there's always war, and I'd like to say this to your Honour," he went on, "'tis many the wet dirty road and crooked lane we travelled together, and 'tis many the whip-lash you've laid on me for speaking and you thinking, and 'tis many's the time you've kicked me awake at two in the morning when the wandering fit was on you; but I'm sorry to leave your Honour, I am so."

"And 'tis many's the guinea of mine you've stolen, sergeant, and many's the nick you've put in my face and your hand jigging while shaving me, with the horrors of drink, and you've worn the good shirts, sergeant, and left me with the torn ones, but I'm sorry to see you go, sergeant."

"God bless your Honour," said the sergeant, "and your Honour's lady. I'll be hitting the road." He took the pieces of a fife from the tail pocket of the long blue coat, screwed them together, took a pull at the faded red facings, cocked his grenadier hat.

"Good luck keep step with you, Sergeant Murphy," said Raftery.

The sergeant wheeled about. His long back straightened. He put the fife to his mouth.

"Some speak of Alexander,
And some of Hercules,"

59

shrilled the grenadier march. He swung back toward Galway City.

> "Of Hero and Leander,
>   And ancients such as these—"

Hilaria watched the stiff straight figure march down the white road. There was a half-sad smile in her eyes and on her mouth.

"O Raftery," she said softly, "how do people live ever in houses?"

But Raftery had found his reins and was swinging into his saddle.

"I can hear the chiming of Lake Corrib," he said, "and the whispering rushes. And they are miles away, Hilaria."

"O Raftery," she said, "let us go. I feel a wind from the mountains on my face."

"It is from the high mountains of Connemara and from the hills of the Joyces' country, little foreign lady."

"O Raftery, let us go."

They passed northward through the lines of the hawthorn hedges that were bursting into great pillars of white spray, where the soft nests of the robin and the bishop wren, and the thrush and blackbird lay in sanctuary, and under the hedges were scattered great clusters of primroses, like handfuls of gold thrown carelessly on the grass, and here were the hosts of bluebells, that were not flowers at all, but the ghosts of flowers, so light, so delicate, so hazily blue, and against the green of the fields, green as green banners, the daisy spread her dainty petticoat and the buttercup flaunted its glazed orange leaf. They rode northward, a queer compelling procession, the greying bronze man with the empty eyes and the lined powerful face, the easy seat, the feet home in the stirrups, the hand on the mare's mouth light as a child's. And beside him on the small black Connemara pony rode the Spanish lady with the glossy hair and the little lace kerchief on it, the face some master puppet-maker would have loved, the delicate white and rose of it, the long crescent of eyebrow and the lashes like fringes of black lace, the narrow curved mouth, and the hands on the reins like resting butterflies, and the shoe like the shoe of some small statue. And behind these two came the great grey shaggy wolf-dog, high as a man's waist, and with fierce proud eyes— about his neck was a collar of bronze and on it, in the Irish letter, "*Cu an Reachtaire*," Raftery's Hound. And then at a little distance the saffron-kilted, saffron-tuniced gillie, with the fighter's slouch, and the lead rein of the packhorse, strong and patient, over his arm. Northward they rode past the flowering hedges and the painted fields. And two great tears dropped through the black fringes of Hilaria's eyes, and rolled down her small cheeks. Raftery turned to her.

"Why do you cry, Hilaria?"

"Because of the summer that is here, Raftery, dark poet and that you cannot see the greenness of the fields, or the flowers how they are white and yellow, or the blossom of the hawthorn gushing forth like a fountain."

"There is little I miss, Hilaria. I can remember them as a child before the plague came on Ireland and I was not blind. And if I wish, too, I can put a screen in my head and see them against it, with all the wonder of a child's wide eyes. But I do not even need that, Hilaria, for a magic comes over me and I am one with them all. The bluebells that quiver in the wind make their minute music in my heart, and I know the daisy how good-hearted she is, and I smile at the flaunting vanity of the rose. And there are scents and sounds that I know the seeing people never have, the scent of rushes and the scent of grass. And the weeds none notice, I know their small virtues.

"And the trees speak to me in the wind. I know the soft dignified music of the ash, and the cheery chatter of the oak-tree, and I know the sad music of the rowan-tree, which has berries red and bitter as some splendid defeated woman's mouth. And the sally-tree that is shy and will only whisper, and out of which are made harps, so sweet it is, harps of red sally-wood.

"And the winds, too, they talk, Hilaria. The wind that comes from the south, and tells of fragrant lands and copper-coloured men, and flowering trees, and fruit with grotesque shapes, as the pineapple. And the northeast wind, coming down from the arctic lands through high-mountained wide-meadowed Ulster, tells of the immense frozen plains, where roam the white bear and the silver fox, and the fat pleasant Laplanders drive in sleighs pulled by reindeer through the slow-falling snow. And the wind from the west blusters and boasts and speaks of great shaggy buffaloes and slim murderous red-skinned men and serpents that rattle and strike. And out of the east comes a mournful cold wind that tells of dead gods and dead creeds, and of dead kings in great pyramids, and of how great Greece sickened and greater Rome fell.

"And I can lie in the heather, Hilaria, and the ancient heather speaks casually of bygone forgotten centuries: of the slim brave men from Africa who were here once, and how out of warm forest and shaggy morass a great evil came on them, and they coughed, and a terror came into their unbeaten eyes, and they died fighting the air with their short heavy swords. And at times the heather speaks of the lumbering, red-bearded, heavy-drinking Danes.

"And close to the earth in the darkness, Hilaria, I can hear the earth's heart beating, the warm generous heart of the earth pulse with the strokes of a round brazen bell."

"Shall I ever hear that, Raftery? Know the song the trees sing and hear the heart," she whispered, "of our mother, the earth?"

"Some night of June, Hilaria, when the little moon is dying in the west, I will take you to a heather-glade, and we will rest by some little copse of hazel-trees, and my left arm will be about your shoulder and your right hand in my right hand, and the tall slim hazel will speak with you, Hilaria, and under the purple coverlet of the heather, Hilaria, you will feel our mother move in her sleep."

"Lord, my Lord Raftery, I am not worthy," she whispered to herself.

They came to Lough Corrib, and skirting it went northward. The sun, that had perched on Raftery's right shoulder as they started, was now low on his left hand. The lapping of the lake waters had the note of evening in it, the quiet note that brings a tune to its close. Soon would come the soft blue twilight, and the lake water turn to a purple that would be almost black, where later would be reflected the steel-blue stars and the money-white moon. And the animals of the hills would come to drink there, the red deer of the antlers, and the hare of the long ears, the uncouth grey badger, and the flaunting rufous fox. Beneath him Raftery felt the white mare tire.

"Hilaria," he asked, "will you for this night sleep under the stars?"

"Dear Raftery," she answered, "to-night of all nights it would irk me to be under a builded roof."

"There will be the wind of summer out," he told her, "and there will be a moon that is all but full, and you will hear the hare in the long grass, and the little creatures of the woods come to drink of the lake.

"Boy"—he called the gillie—"water and picket the horses. Get fire-wood from the lake shore. And near this place there should be a strong farmer's house."

"Sir, there is blue smoke a mile down the road."

"Whatever you need for a meal and haven't got, go there and find it, warm farls of bread, new milk, China tea."

"Sir," asked the boy, "do I buy or steal?"

"They may give it to you, because we are travellers. If they don't, offer them money. If they part for neither money nor charity, tell them you are Patrick Raftery's man."

"Raftery"—Hilaria took his sleeve—"will you come apart with me for a little while."

He walked with her over the road. Beneath his feet was the springy heather. In his face was the warmth of the setting sun. He walked on, her fingers on his sleeve. And still the sun was in his face, and now he heard the soughing of the rowan-trees.

"There is a great stone here, Raftery," she said. "Will you sit down?"

He sat on the shaggy grey boulder, and she sank on her knees beside him. With her

66

sweet bowed head and her hands on her bosom, she was like a Madonna in an ancient beloved church. She knelt there silent as a stone Madonna. But her face was to the sun and her heart was to it. And Raftery could feel the swift flight of her prayer. Toward the sun she was praying, as if she wanted to wash her heart in it, to plunge her soul into its flaming depths. Even when he put his hand upon her bowed shoulder, he could feel the urge of her body towards it, as if it wanted to bathe in the molten purifying furnace, in the great fiery cleansing depths of the sun.

And after a little while he could feel heart and soul and body cohering, coalescing again. And her voice came to him with a note of wonder.

"Patrick Raftery," she said, "tell me, are we two, of a surety, on the road to the county of Mayo?"

"We are on that road, Hilaria."

"And will it be as you said in the poem on the quay-side, Raftery?"

"In all sweet Ireland," he told her, "there is no sweeter county than County Mayo."

"Will there ever be any more of that poem, Raftery?"

"There will always be more of it.   There is more of it now.   Listen, Hilaria:

"Hilaria will cross her hands upon her breast,
    And kneeling dimly in the soft blue air,
Out of her heart she will send into the burning west,
    A cool sweet prayer.

Robbing the plover's nest for her small eggs, and the
       wild bee's hoard for his honey,
    And netting the fat gold-spangled trout from the
       frosty mountain stream,
With China tea and white farls we buy for the smallest
       silver money,
    We shall eat and dream.

"And wait in the Irish twilight for the high moon that is
       late in coming,
    And nothing shall break in to unquiet the deep warm
       peace,
But the call of a distant eagle, or the bittern's drum-
       ming,
    Or the shrill wild geese . . ."

CHAPTER VIII

So they went northward still past lake and river, going through townlands and villages which had names in the Irish language, if you knew the Irish language, that would bring a warm picture to your eye and heart: as Srajcua, a lane between whitewashed, barley-thatched houses, and cherry woods on each side of it, and green meadows lush with grass, and the name of that in English is the Cuckoos' Street. In summer in that village from every art and part the cuckoos call one to another, so that one might think there was nothing but flutes and oboes in the cherry woods. And they went through Park na Mla Derg, which means the Plain of Red Flowers, such a great wide carpet of poppies spread over that demesne, and the folk of the village are a drowsy peaceful people. And they passed Kooig Meela Free, which is Five Miles of Heather, and there is a silken wind blowing over that townland, blowing the honeyed scent of the purple heather to the homesick people over all the world. That townland is a favourite place of the fairies, so if you have business with the little people of the hills you can always find them at Five Miles of Heather, when they gather for the piping and the stone-throwing contests and other athletic events in August under the full moon. And they passed the townland of Kranna Arigid, Silver Trees, where the breeze keeps the leaves of birch and hazel in a shimmer, so that in the moonlight you would have good reason for thinking you had come to Tir nan Og. And the clusters of hazel-nuts in Kranna Arigid are the largest and richest in all the Irish nation, brown clusters in small green fronds.

And they stopped at the village of Dherran Dhoun, which means the End of the World, for there begin the Mountains of Connemara, and there is nothing but the high purple peaks between this village and the Atlantic Sea, and the name was put on this village before Columbus discovered the Americas, so that in olden times it was a good name, and I have heard it argued that it is a good name still. They stopped at Bartholomew Joyce's drinking-house, where there is good trade. And in the sanded public room Raftery with his cloak about his face listened to the news of the day. A Longford pig-buyer, a stocky man with a great horseshoe moustache, and a long whip in his left hand and a pot of porter in his right, was telling how Dean Swift had come back to Dublin from England last month in great anger, and why:

". . . so my bold man walks straight into Hampton's Courthouse, and pushes every one aside until he comes to where Queen Anne is sitting, all by herself.

"'Och, dean, my jewel,' she says, 'and how are you?'

"'Less of the how-are-you, ma'am,' says the dean, 'and more about this: have you e'er a bishop's apron and gaiters that would fit me, and if you haven't, why haven't you?'

"'I have better than that, dean, my darling,' says Queen Anne. 'How,' says she, 'would you like to marry me?'

"'I wouldn't like it at all,' says the dean.

"'And why not?' says the queen, says she.

"'For three reasons, ma'am,' says he. 'The first is: St. Paul says, those who marry do well, but those who don't do better.'

"'And did I think I'd live to see the day,' says Queen Anne, 'when a six-foot Irishman would bother about what a cantankerous old lad like that would say! And didn't he also say,' she asked him, for she's the grand Bible-reading old girl, 'that 'tis better to marry than burn? Ah, dean,' she told him, 'your second reason will have to be better.'

"'My second is this,' he said; 'if so be I went back to Dublin, and me married to the queen of England, I'd scorn to tell you what they'd do to me, but you can get a hint from this, that my head would be kicking around the liberties of Dublin, and someone in Belfast would be poking the fire with my shin-bone, and my entrails would be fertilizing the county of Cork.'

"'Och, dean,' she said, 'my loving man, what need for you to go back to Dublin when you can stay here in Hampton's Courthouse and sit in your ease in the parlour, with a quart of whisky at your elbow and write your Sullivan's Travels. And the Life Guards there to keep out them as do be annoying the poets——publishers, and policeman, and people with bills. And the queen of England making tea for you with her royal hands. What's your third reason, dean dear?' she asked, 'for them two's no good.'

"'My third reason is, that I'm married already. Ah,' he said, 'I thought that'd hold you.'

"For the queen lets a screech out of her you could hear a mile away, and falls into the megrims, and her women came running to her with violet-water and orange-water and lavender-water and plain water in a bucket, for the queen was a teetotaler. But all she does is screech: 'Put the dirty devil out.'

"'Ma'am,' says the dean, '*pogue ma hone*, which is Irish for: the back of my hand to ye.' And back to Dublin he comes, leaping with anger."

"But I never heard tell," said Bartholomew Joyce, "that the dean was married."

"May I never destroy another pint of porter," said the Longford pig-buyer, "if I'm telling a lie. For he's married to a girl in the County Kildare, and when he's with her he hates her and can't bear the sight of her, and when he's away from her he sits up all night writing her letters saying how much he loves her, letters as long as a road without a public house." And the pig-buyer inserted skilfully the horseshoe moustache into the foaming pot of porter. . . .

But from another man Raftery received more authentic information on the times. He was a squat, fat, bald-faced man, with a neck wrinkled like a turtle's, a droning conventicle voice, black suit, and black slouch hat. He had come into Connaught to preach the approaching coming of Christ and the millennium. The wicked, he announced, would be swept with the besom of destruction.

"And they are wicked, brother," he told Raftery. "I came on the flying canal-boat from Dublin to the town of Athlone, and such drinking on board, such consumption of brandy and wine, such lascivious dancing, as the tarantella, that lewdness of Italy. Oh, fie, fie, brother! And the merchants of repute such as Master Dafydd Evans with his painted Spanish concubine. Oh, shameless, brother! The shew of their countenance doth witness against them," he chanted, "and they declare their sin as Sodom; they hide it not. A popish woman and a harlot, brother!"

"I would much rather you did not call me brother," said Raftery quietly, "though you may be a very worthy man. But when does your millennium come?"

"It comes now, brother;" the preacher paid no attention to his request. "There will be no more wars, and for all there will be gold and silver, shekels of gold and shekels of silver. For is it not written that the wolf also shall dwell with the lamb, and the weaned

child shall put his hand on the cockatrice his
den? Is it not in Holy Script, brother?"

"I will not dispute what is written with you,
for there are many foolish things written,
including some by myself. But how does
this come about, my man?"

"As all things come about, brother, by the
grace of God and the labour of virtuous men.
There has been formed in London, brother, a
company of godly and cunning merchants
called the South Sea Company, whose aim
is to develop the trade of the South Seas.
There is wealth past dreaming there, brother,
golden sands and hills of diamonds, which
the ignorant heathen will part with for a
handful of glass beads or some tin gewgaw.
Oh, our day has arrived, brother, as arrived
the day of Spain, when the Americas were
given her to plunder, and the day of Tyre
and Sidon, whose merchants were princes,
whose traffickers were the honourable of the
earth. We are neither a heathen nor a popish
nation, brother. Prosperity will abide with
our godly breed. Already," he whispered,
"the shares of the South Sea Company have
risen two hundred per centum, and they are
to be bought even in this most ignorant
province of Connaught."

'From the Welshman of Claregalway, perhaps," sneered Raftery.

"No, no," the preacher said, "for his iniquities and abominations Master Dafydd Evans has been blinded with ignorance. The stars of heaven and the constellations thereof shall not give him their light. He sniffeth disaster from afar, and saith ha-ha! No, brother, they are to be had from me, from me alone."

Hilaria's little feet came over the sanded floor. She laid her hand on Raftery's shoulder.

"All is ready in our room, Raftery," she said. "Do you wish to take the dust of travel off?"

But the preacher was upon his feet.

"I have seen this woman before," he shrilled. "I have seen her on the flying canal-boat. She is the Spanish hussy who brought Master Dafydd Evans to the mire. O brother, brother."

"You are mistaken, worthy man," said Raftery gently. "You have never before insulted this lady by looking at her with your pig's eyes."

"O brother, brother, beware of false witness and lying, and especially beware of this woman, for her feet go down to death, her steps take hold in hell."

76

"Religious sir," said Raftery, "you are a most damned liar."

"Who are you, to speak to me in this way?" the preaching man shouted.

"I am Patrick Raftery"—and Raftery turned his face full on the room—"the chief poet of the Irish people; and this is my wife, Hilaria."

There was a hush and quick chatter in the room, but the clergyman was beside himself with anger.

"You are a rogue," he shouted, "an impertinent penniless fellow!"

"O Bartholomew Joyce," said Raftery quietly, "have I honoured your house, only to be insulted by this lewd Anabaptist?"

There was a growl in the room, and Raftery swept Hilaria close to him to avoid the rush as tables and chairs were overturned, and a torrent of feet poured over the sanded floor.

"Don't kill him," Raftery said.

He could hear the man howl as he was hauled through the door, howl as he was pitched into the village pond, howl as he rushed up the hills like a frightened stoat from the village called Dherran Dhoun which is in English the End of the World, for there is nothing between that village and the green Atlantic surges but the wilderness of the purple Connemara hills.

CHAPTER IX

I

As they went northward through the sleeping Connaught towns, May gave way to June, the blue of the barley took a faint, a very faint gold as yet, that later would be white as a child's head. The scythes swished through the tall grass, and there came to the nostrils the scent of mown hay and wild bees' honey. The blue road reared and slid and twisted, and great purple mountain was followed by small black lake. Some days the sun would shine merrily as a piper plays, and on other days a great dignity would come on him, and he would shine steadily as a great ship moves, ripening the meadows of clover and the broad fields of barley. And on other days he would not be visible, and broad sheets of fine Irish rain, gentle and light as feathers, would sweep the hills while they rode on, Hilaria wrapped in the great blue Irish cloak, her face peeping

from its cowl like the face of a small dark
child; the brown face of Raftery brooding
like some brown streaming boulder that
broods upon the mists and hills. And on
other days great boisterous gusts of wind
would be out screaming and roaring around
the shoulders of the mountains and racing
over the plains, tang of salt sea and heather on
them; lurching, curving, playful winds, that
would make man and woman light-headed and
reckless and gay. They skirted the shore of
Lough Mask and in the distance saw Lough
Conn.

But in every village they passed there was
not the hearty welcome Raftery used to find.
There was courtesy and hospitality, but the
people were not so light-hearted as he remembered them to have been or so free with him.
And everywhere, which he did not see, were
harsh cold glances at Hilaria, and sometimes
whispering against her. And there were men
who had laughter in their faces, until they
felt the cold grey eye of the Scottish gillie on
them, and noticed him finger playfully the
hilt of his knife. In front of these people
Hilaria's head was proud and high, but when
she was away from them, her white chin would
fall, and a cloud would come in her eyes.

And she saw, which Raftery did not see, many a gentleman, riding toward them, put his horse at a ditch when he noticed them coming. And once an Irish lady rode toward and past them, surrounded by armed clansmen, and gave them neither "God bless you!" nor "May your road be lucky!"

"Was she who passed," asked Raftery slowly, "a slender haughty woman, with black hair, and grey eyes?"

"She was not, please your Honour," lied the gillie, "but a fair-haired fat English-woman, with no manners at her, and ignorant in the face."

"It is strange," said Raftery. "I have known only one woman with the scent of apples from her, and that was Lady Barbara Butler, who was close to me, and I young."

They rode northward still, hearing in the village inns the news of the day, of how Lord Clare was dead in France, and of the opening of Parliament in Dublin, and everywhere talk of the money that was being made in the shares of the South Sea Company, and of how queer it was that the Welshman of Claregalway was taking no interest in the scheme, he that had the cunning of a ferret when it came to money. 'Twas a strange thing surely, "but maybe," it was suggested, "they wouldn't let him have a share in it at all, at all, the South Sea Company being merchants of high degree and he having a name dirtier than a tinker's."

But they ran into more pleasant things than histories of the corruption of Parliament, and of the exile of the Dillons, and of how money can be made. Coming into Greenan Neeya, the Sunny Place of the Red Deer, they heard a blind piper, with a bellows of chased silver and silver stops on his reed, playing a tune with a great lilt to it. He was sitting on a bench outside a small whitewashed house, and the sun shone warmly on his pathetic face and empty eyes.

"What tune is that you have, man of the pipes?" Raftery called, "for 'tis a new tune to me."

"'Tis a tune of my own making, your Honour," the piper said, "founded on a country poem of the great Irish poet's, Patrick Raftery."

"'Tis 'The Fair of Ballinderry,' so?"

"'Tis, your Honour."

"What is it?" asked Hilaria.

"It's only doggerel, Hilaria."

"'Tis not doggerel at all, your Honour," objected the piper, "but a grand rural poem,

with a fine picture and swing in it, and some
most intricate rimes."

"May I hear it, piper?" Hilaria asked.
"I should feel happy to hear that poem."

"God bless your ladyship's sweet voice,"
said the piper. "Indeed you shall hear that
poem. 'Tis how it goes this way:

"'Tis pretty to be in Ballinderry!
'Tis pretty to be in Aghadee!
'Tis pretty to be in Little Ram's Island,
Sitting under an ivy-tree!

"On the day of the fair in Ballinderry,
From every county the cadgers come;
The dealing men who are whisky merry;
The recruiting sergeant with his fife and drum.
Pigs are trotting in grunting battalions;
And small brown donkeys patiently browse,
Under the heels of beribboned stallions,
Dodging the horns of the Kerry cows.
'Take it or leave it,' the farmers are shouting,
'And five pounds more, or be damned to you!'
While in the boxers' tents the bruisers are clouting
The country fighters black and blue.
A Gipsy woman is telling the fortune
Of some thick gaping servant-girl,
Promising her without land or portion
A castle in England and a healthy earl.
A slut is cursing a man who repulsed her,
Impeaching himself and his pedigree;

And claiming in all fair-womaned Ulster,
None is her beating for gentility.
A cloud of sheep come to scatter the cattle,
And all is deavened by the drover's noise,
But the cheers and groans that mark the battle
Between Clann O'Loughlin and the Regan boys.
Down by the pond the Belfast Dandy
Is 'telling the story' to some village youth,
And steering him off for a glass of brandy
To Molly Brannagan's drinking-booth.
And all the money of the ploughman's pay-day
Is taken from him by the gaming coves,
With 'trick of the loop,' and 'find the lady,'
And voices gentle as a wooing dove's.
On the village green the couples are tilting,
Merrily tapping with toe and heel,
Against each other to the bagpipe's lilting,
In 'The Walls of Limerick' and 'The Four Hand Reel.'

"Ah, I wish I were in Ballinderry,
And I wish to God my poor eyes could see
The blossoming boughs of Little Ram's Island,
And the hundred houses of Aghadee."

"My lady, that is the fair of Ballinderry, as
a blind man would see it, the queer wee picture
in his head, the shouts of the dealers, the
lilting of the union pipes, the patter of dancing.
And the four wee lines at the end of it, m'lady,
that is the cry of the blind man. For the
Raftery is blind, too, m'lady, since the small-

83

pox spread black wings over Ireland and plucked out our eyes."

"You have never seen Raftery?"

"Sure, how could I, m'lady, and no eyes at me? But I can figure him in my mind, a powerful kindly man with an eagle's face."

"Blind man," said Hilaria softly, "this with me is the Raftery."

"Oh, my lady"—the piper's face quivered—"you wouldn't be mocking a poor blind man. . . . But I would know him if he would let me touch his hand."

Raftery slipped down from his saddle and put his arm around the old man's shoulder.

"Yes, it is I, brother."

"Asthore Na Erin," the piper wept, "Ireland's darling, sure I thought the day I met you my pipes would peal like an organ, but now they're like me, dark poet, ashamed and dumb. . . ."

II

It was at Boor Na Mocka, the Cadger's Road, that the little party were overtaken by the peddling man. He was a blackavised short greasy fellow riding on a mule, with a peddler's pack behind him, and in his eyes was a store of evil knowledge. He had a soft fawning smile, and wary eyes.

"It is Raftery, the great poet," he shouted. "May I die if it is not great Raftery!" And Raftery had to manœuvre the white mare forward to avoid clasping hands.

"But it is a shame," he cried, "great Raftery with his hands bare as if he were a working man. Not a ring, not a diamond! Who would know you were a great poet? I have here in this pack a diamond ring——" Raftery waved him aside. But he would not be daunted.

"Great Raftery," he whispered hoarsely, "you have probably got a great deal of money on you, offerings and presents and fees. There is danger on the road; you may be murdered for them. Now, I have with me some stock of the great South Sea Company, which is better, may I die! than money, and safer, Raftery, to carry around, for thieves will not rob you of papers. They are easily traced; see, Raftery! And the shares will go up, Raftery, up to the sky."

"I have little money," Raftery answered wearily, "and little desire for riches. Packman, please leave me be."

They were passing, on the great lonely road, the wide pool known as Pollgon Thone, the Hole without a Bottom. A cold nor'west wind blew toward them on their left-hand side and rippled the dark waters, and the reeds quivered with the stark breeze.

"But something you will buy for the pretty lady, eh, great Raftery? A present for the pretty lady," he leered at Hilaria. "I know the ways of pretty ladies. They like presents, a ring for a slim finger or a bracelet for a soft arm, or a pair of gold spurs for delicate riding-boots."

"I want nothing," said Hilaria.

"I know you, pretty lady," said the peddler. "I have seen you in Dublin, at the theatre in Fishamble Lane, pretty lady, and in St. Stephen's Green, when the gentlemen walk to take the air, each with his pretty lady on his arm——"

"Have you, indeed?" said Hilaria, carelessly, coldly.

"Merchant," said Raftery courteously, "we are but poor company on the road, madam and I. We are a silent pair, madam and I. So we will ride ahead, merchant, and good luck to you with your wares." And they rode on. The peddling man stood by the great pool, his face dark with anger.

"So that is the way!" he called after they had ridden a little distance. "A decent merchant is not good enough company for a penny poet. Anybody with a copper to spare can have your poems, cheap Raftery, and madam!" he laughed. "Madam she calls herself now. A great pair," he called out loudly after them. "A ha'penny Irish poet and the Welshman of Claregalway's whore——"

The wind whirled his words away, so that only the gillie, leading the packhorse after them, heard him. He slung the reins on the horse's back and returned with quick slouching steps. The packman watched the saffron tunic and kilt hustle toward him and became sick with fear.

"Hands off, yellow-belly," he screamed.

Quickly and painlessly his end came. The lad's right hand flashed upward toward the gullet with the broad knife, and there was a splash as he was whirled from the mule's back into the black bog water. . . . The mule fled down the road.

Raftery galloped up on the grey mare. "What is wrong, boy?" he asked. "A black wing touched my face."

"'Tis this poor peddling man," said the

gillie, "fell from his mule, and there is neither sight nor sign of him in the bog water. They are treacherous things, the mules, please your Honour."

"Help me off with my clothes, boy," Raftery said. "I'll try for him."

"You will not, please your Honour, but myself am like a seal in the water, and I'll go. But there is little hope, please your Honour, for this is the Pollgon Thone."

He slipped out of kilt and tunic, and went into the water with the soft plunge of an otter. His white body disappeared in the black depths. He dived again and again.

"I can find neither bottom nor packman, please your Honour, and I feel the swish of great flippers near me, and I in the depths. But I'll try once more."

"Come out, lad," Raftery called after a little while. "You have done your duty."

"Indeed, sir," the boy answered grimly as he scrambled upon the grass, "if your Honour will allow me to praise myself, I have so."

CHAPTER X

I

BUILDED now was the leafy house of June. Each tree was dressed like a young girl for a dance. Sleek silken leaves of the sally, and proud head of the rowan-tree, and the copper beech with the tawny locks of a woman; the flaunting candles of the horse-chestnut; the elm's sweet simplicity. And here and there were great purple rocks, and now townlands fertile as gold—great fields of rye and barley, and rolling plains of clover whence came the minute thunder of bees. The pretty flowers and tall blue stalk of the bean gave forth their gentle perfume. And overhead fluttered the meadow-larks, pouring down their cataract of song.

About Raftery and Hilaria was the short sweet grass of downs. Beneath them ran high cliffs to where the murmuring mad Atlantic lurched and rolled in ponderous banner-green waves, black fighting cliffs with here and there a fissure where bloomed some gnome's garden, maidenhair ferns and delicate mosses, the chiming blue of the harebell, the saxifrage and silver silene, and daisies with crimson petals, great sprays of honeysuckle, all cunningly protected from the salt breeze and sea. And near them on the downs was a cluster of beehive cells, where monks of more than a thousand years before had dwelt in the odour of sanctity and honeysuckle, following the gentle rule of Brendan and Brigid, and of Columkill.

The gillie had brought the harp out to the cliffs, where Raftery wished to tune it and see that all was ready in preparation for a coming tour.

"For vulgar as it sounds, small Hilaria," he told her, "I must make a little money, so I shall polish up the planxties and add a new verse or two to 'The Green Woods of Truagh' and to 'The County of Mayo.'"

"What need, Lord Raftery?" she asked.

"I have heard a religious well-fed man once tell," he laughed, "of a prophet, Elijah to wit, who was fed by ravens. But this is June, small Hilaria, and the glossy Irish crows do not gather until the brown leaves fall. And

moreover, what may have been excellent
feeding for this worthy Hebrew may be poor
fare to an Irish poet, and an Irish poet's
lady."

"So you must go, then." Her face was
white, her small mouth twisted.

Very reverently the gillie put down the
harp and took from it the cover of poplin silk
that swathed it, and set its gold and silver and
red sally-wood glinting in the morning sun.
"*Ego sum regina cithararum*," it proudly said
on the *lamhchrann* or front pillar in silver
letters, "I am the queen of the harps." About
it a great tradition hung: that it had been made
for Shane O'Neill and that he had played the
airs of Ulster on it for Elizabeth the queen.
The Red Hand of Ulster was blazoned in
crimson and gold beneath the proud Latin
proclamation, and under that in Irish:
"Donough MacShane made me. Gialla
Christ Fitz Patrick was my musician and
harmonist, and if there were a better, him
should I have had: Dermot Ward along with
him, two highly accomplished men, whom I
had to nurse me; and may God have mercy
on them all!" And here and there were
inscriptions in Gaelic, "The Yellow Ford!"
and one could hear in the high air the ring of

the Ulster steel. And here was a pathetic signature scrawled with the point of a dagger: "Pierce Ferriter moriturus." "Now Pierce Ferriter dies!" And one could see the warrior-bishop facing his butchers on that cold morning in Killarney. Wolf-dogs were wrought in red gold, along the *corr* or harmonic curve, and the screws of silver and sounding-holes ornamented with silver flashed in the sunshine of the county of Mayo.

"O Raftery!" Hilaria breathed in wonder. "It was given me," said Raftery, "by Walpurga Butler. She was a very old lady, Hilaria, one hundred and eight years old when she died, and she spoke only Latin and the Irish tongue. She gave it to me on her death-bed because I had written a bitter poem about the loss of my eyes. She told me any tinker of the road could have two eyes, but only a poet and a gentleman could have the Clanrickarde harp. Her only fear in dying, Hilaria, was that God might have become slightly common, through having so many middle-class saints about Him."

But Hilaria never even smiled. She heard him, but her eyes were on the green Atlantic, that growled and thundered at the foot of the cliffs. Afar off the seagulls soared and wept, and not three knots from land were the orange sails of the fishing-boats. Southward a great ship heeled under a white pyramid of sail.

"I wish I were a good harper," Raftery was musing, "for the sake of the harp itself. But all I can do, Hilaria, is mark the rhythm of poems with the booming strings." He swept his hand over the chords, and suddenly the leashed life of the harp bounded into the clean air, as a red deer springs forward, or a swan jumps in the month of May. Raftery laid his cheek beside the pillar as the notes fluttered like birds over the wind-swept cliffs:

"Whoever saw Hilaria," [he chanted gently], "walk down
      the Cuckoos' Street,
   Saw a slim tree of brown hazel pass on silver feet;
   Saw the white moon of April on her slight third day;
   Saw green waves dance, as queens dance, into Galway
      Bay."

"O Raftery, don't!" She became red with modesty and embarrassment. "Please, dear Raftery, don't."

But the harp crashed into a rhythm that was like the gallop of racing horses, the smooth striding measure of great thorough-bred horses:

"Whoever saw Hilaria ride through Ogonello,
  Saw blue shadows sweep the mountains when the sun
    is low;
  Saw the royal salmon springing up the grass-grown
    weir;
  Whoever saw Hilaria," [he sang gently], "saw a swift
    red deer."

Her face was clouded with tears. Her throat was choking. She put out a feeble remonstrating hand. The harp changed to a high note, like a young boy singing in some vast church:

"Whoever saw Hilaria through Knockbeg pass,
  Saw Mary, Christ's mother on the patient ass—"

"Raftery, please Raftery, don't," she sobbed.

Led by meek bearded Joseph," [the song went on
    inexorably], "who guided them,
  Toward a manger in the city of cold Bethlehem."

She stood white and taut now, and her voice came firmly. "O Patrick Raftery," she cried, "hear me."
He leaned his arms on the harmonic curve of the queen of harps. His bronzed concentrated face was toward her, his eyes were hooded, as hawks' eyes are, so that no

man could have judged there was no sight
there.

"I hear you, Hilaria."

"O Raftery, you married me without asking
me whose daughter I was, or what condition
of life I was in."

"Why should I ask, Hilaria? I heard you
one evening sing 'The Girls of Cadiz,' and
Fate laid his hand on my shoulder. Troubled
Hilaria, had I married a woman of the shee,
should I ask of her the secrets of the fairy
people?"

"Do not fence with me, Patrick Raftery.
You know very well that none can understand
a person without knowing what background
they stand against. Without that the person
is but a symbol in a riddle one has not the
body of. You know that, great poet."

"I know that, Hilaria."

She sank down on the short sweet grass.
Her white hands clasped her small supple
knees.

"O Raftery," she asked, "is it true that the
swan sings a song and dies?"

"I heard the chief swan of the Shannon
die," Raftery remembered. "It was on a
winter night, with a full moon in it, and I
making eastward toward central Ireland. It

rose on vast wings past me, Hilaria, and when it was high in the air it sang its great song to the winter moon. It was the proud song of an organ, Hilaria, and in it the lapping of lake water and the wind among the rushes, and the song of all the little birds at sunrise was in it, and the sun and the moon themselves. And then he folded his wings and dropped like a stone into the waters; and where the Shannon carried him, Hilaria, I do not know. But it was months before I could touch the harp again, such music was there in the chief swan's song."

"I can sing no song, Raftery, but I will tell you a story, and when that is told I shall die, Raftery, as the chief swan died"—she looked toward the cliffs—"hurtling through the clear Connaught air, for I was always," she said, "an eagle or great swan in my heart and mind."

His hand found the bass strings of the harp, and began plucking out the air Carolan had composed for "The Green Woods of Truagh" the faint thunder of the wood-pigeons in the silken emerald leaves.

"Yes, Hilaria?" he said.

"O Raftery," she leaned forward, "see Spain!"

"I see a harsh good country," said Raftery, "like a harsh good wine. Gaunt rocks and trees that are all but black, so green they are, cool houses, Hilaria, a burning dazzling sun, and a cool hardy wind."

"See an old house with a deep well near it, and vineyards in terraces, Raftery."

"I see, Hilaria."

She leaned forward in concentration.

"Can you see a small dark woman, smaller than I, Raftery, with a Moorish unconquerable look, and small feet that twinkle as they move? She is dead, Raftery. She died when I was eight years old."

"The green terraces of Heaven are hers, Hilaria."

"And can you see a tall broad-shouldered man, as tall and broad-shouldered as any in the Irish country? A great all-but-giant of a man, with the face of an eagle, and beautiful manners, and, Raftery, beaten eyes. He is dead."

"There died a gentleman," said Patrick Raftery.

"He was my father, and the little woman was my mother, and the Welshman of Clare-galway held our lands in fee."

"Must you tell me, Hilaria?"

"I must, Patrick Raftery. When my father died, the Welshman of Claregalway put me in a convent at his own expense. The Welshman had drinking-shops in Bristol City for the sailors from foreign ports, and that is why he had liens on vineyards in France and Spain. But the Welshman is a queer man, Raftery, for he is forever making deals with God. And because of some monstrous unspeakable treachery he had done elsewhere, he paid for me at school. But the Welshman is a trickster, Raftery; he went back on his bargain with God.

"When I was sixteen the Welshman of Claregalway came to see me, Raftery, and he took me away.

"And for two years we travelled everywhere, Raftery. But for all he did for me I could not love this man. I could not marry anyone who was like my father, Raftery, for I had no portion. All I could marry was some wretched lout, and that I would not do, Raftery, for I was always an eagle in my heart.

"One day in Spain the Welshman sent for me and recounted the money he had spent on me, and named the price of everything I wore, from the high comb in my hair to the red shoes upon my feet. 'And why do I spend this money, Hilaria?' he asked.

"'Sir, because you love me as a daughter,' I said.

"'I love you, but not as a daughter.'

"'Then you wish to marry me,' I said.

"'I do not spend money on a woman I would marry,' he told me. 'I would get money with her. No, I have bought you, Hilaria.'

"I thought: He is a business man. He has spent money for a return, and I have used it. I didn't know, but that is business.

"'Have your money's worth then, Welsh-man,' I said.

"And that night, Raftery," she said bravely, "the Welshman of Claregalway came into my sleeping-room.

"What would you have me do?" she cried passionately. "Kill myself, as the women in stories do? Does that solve anything? Run away? Whither, then? Without money, without friends, to end up in some townsmen's bagnio? What should I do?"

"I would have you do nothing, Hilaria," said Raftery gently, "but work out your own destiny."

"So I was in pawn to the Welshman of Claregalway," she said, "for three long years.

"But that was not what was wrong, Raftery. This is where wrong lies, that I never surrendered the eagle's heart. I was like some young eagle that had been caught by stratagem and was chained by the claw to the door-step of some vulgar man's house. And I knew, as the eagle knows, that one day the chain will break, and that again he will soar over the snowy mountains and look in the sun's eye. Though captivity has broken his heart and his wings are weakened by years of the burgess's chain, yet if only for a moment he will rise and gaze proudly at the sun.

"And I thought: One day the Welshman of Claregalway will tire of me, and will put me out, having had of me his money's worth and more, and I will marry no slipshod facile man with the luckpenny he throws me, but I will go to where the girls of Cadiz sit like bedizened puppets in their windows when night falls, awaiting the purchaser, and there I will ply the trade the Welshman had taught me, until the hour of the eagle comes. Am I very shameless, Raftery? Do eagles know shame?"

But Raftery said nothing. His hand still wandered carelessly among the strings, now plucking out that part of Carolan's melody that went to his own words, of how once every hundred years, out of an ancient majestic tree in the heart of the green woods of Truagh, comes a silver woman with golden eyes, and in her hand are the two halves of a broken sceptre, and as she walks she weeps, and all the wild things of the woods and mountains weep with her, for she is Maeve the queen, great Maeve, poor conquered Maeve. . . . One might have thought he was not listening, but Hilaria knew he was.

"But, Raftery, my hour came sooner than I thought. For the Welshman of Claregalway used me to hunt you and your great name. Where you are received with honour, the hounds hunt him from the door. And the four lines you made on him stabbed deeper than daggers can.

"And he thought if you married me, there would no longer be welcome for you anywhere. And your name would be a derision, for he has let all the world know I was his bought woman.

"And I, I knew the hour of the eagle had come, and I took it as eagles do, caring little about right or wrong. But, Raftery, the Welshman of Claregalway is caught in his own snare."

"As how, Hilaria?" Raftery asked.

"O Patrick Raftery," she said, "have I been

a good wife to you, this small time in the county of Mayo?"

"You have been a good wife," Raftery answered, "and a true loving friend, and within and without, you are beauty."

"Then listen, Patrick Raftery: my time has not been wasted for you. Now my name is hated by every poor man's drudging wife; but when I am dead, Raftery, there will be about me a mystery and a majesty. A big gesture wipes out small and sordid things, and the Irish nation will forgive me, once I am dead, and what blame there is will be laid at the door of the Welshman of Claregalway, who went back even on his bargain with God. And later, you, too, will forgive, Patrick Raftery, because you are great and wise, and sometimes in the evening when a friend is reading to you from the books and journals of the day, there will come on your face that deep dreaming look I know so well, and you will not be listening to him, but thinking of Hilaria, who wronged you and loved you, Patrick Raftery, and out of your heart, Raftery, which has forgiven me, some fragrant little song may come."

She stood up, and wrapped the gay Spanish shawl about her. She looked forward to the gaunt cliffs beneath which, a hundred fathoms below, the deep green Atlantic growled in long surges and shouldered the land with surly gigantic blows. Her feet moved slowly over the short cliff grass.

"You have the Queen of Harps, Raftery, and you have the love and admiration of the Irish people, and you have your own great gift. And as the years roll on you will have rewards and honours." Her eyes were blinded with tears. "And once, Raftery, an eagle gave you its heart."

"Come hither, Hilaria," Raftery commanded. He stood upright, one hand on the harp. His face was set like some graven face on an ancient coin.

"I said: come hither!" His voice ordered as bugles.

She turned and moved toward him irresolutely. Her mouth twisted. "O Patrick Raftery," she asked, "are you going to kill me?"

"Come hither, Hilaria." His big bronze hand whipped out like the paw of a cat, and gripped her shoulder. His steel-like fingers bit into her soft shoulder, like the claws of some great cat, tiger or leopard or other great forest cat. She did not flinch, but raised her proud tear-stained face to him.

"What do you want of me, Patrick Raftery?"

"O Hilaria," he said gently, "you who are blind, let you open your eyes."

"How, Lord Raftery?"

"When sight was taken from me, Hilaria, I was given a gift: I could sit in one small room and see the world; and the masks folk wear, the golden masks or black mottled masks, deceived me no more. So that the night you sat and sang the song of the girls of Cadiz, Hilaria, your heart was bare. And I knew, Hilaria."

"And you married me, Raftery!" she sobbed. "In spite of that you married me. Oh, why, Patrick Raftery?"

"Do you think I could take a woman to wife, Hilaria, who measured men and things by the shallow measure of the eyes? Listen, Hilaria; we are born and die and then are immortal. But death is not the quiet sleep that comes at the end of life; or the little curtain that falls while we cast off the winter garment of the body, and wander off into June sunshine and singing waters. There is a death that comes to all of us in life, as it came to me when was taken from me the sight of my eyes, as it came to you when the Welshman of Claregalway entered your sleeping-room—and we sit a little while by ourselves in an apart dark place, and we learn truths, of how certain things one believes to be good are but vulgar selfish things, and how certain things the small think evil are but futile accidents. And we learn to be kind; such wisdom comes when we are dead. And those who have never died in life, Hilaria, are pleasant shallow people, soulless as seals. O Hilaria, open your blind eyes."

"But I am soiled, Patrick Raftery."

"Is your mind soiled?"

"My mind is clean and keen as a knife."

"Your heart, Hilaria?"

"My heart had a lock and seal set on it until you came, Raftery. But the Welshman of Claregalway has soiled me, Raftery."

"One can soil only oneself, Hilaria. How little wisdom you have after all, dark child!" She sank on her knees, and the slim sweet body began to shake with sobs. He put his hand on her silky head. "The small eagle's heart drives it crashing against the bars. Hush, small child," he whispered. "You are now in the county of Mayo, where always you wished to be, where the sun is like golden ale, and the turf soft as a swan's breast, and soon there will be soft twilight, Hilaria, and the quiet of God over all the land, the crickets singing and the swift flutter of swallows. And later the lamps will be lit, and the corn-crakes call, and you must dry your eyes, Hilaria, or you cannot read for us when the evening falls."

"O Patrick Raftery, will you have me still?"

"I will have you for ever and ever."

"But the Irish nation, Raftery——"

"Listen, Hilaria," he said, "I have, at one time or another, stood a great deal from the Irish nation, and now the Irish nation will have to stand something from me. For if it comes to parting," he said, "I can do much better without the Irish nation than the Irish nation can do without Patrick Raftery."

II

They were passing by Carra Lake, through the great belts of trees, where the woodcock are so plentiful. There was a coolness under the green trees, and in the lake the pike were swirling. And the little water birds were pattering around the lapping edges on the outlook for unwary minnows. Raftery was walking along with his hand on the wolf-dog's collar. Beside him Hilaria tripped, her shawl like the plumage of some exotic bird, her sweet child's eyes watching the swirling circles in the lake water. Behind them the gillie led the horses. Toward them galloped a heavy farm horse, lumbering like a wagon. On its back was a farmer in knee-breeches and flopping black felt hat, beating the animal on the croup with an ash-plant. When he saw Raftery he pulled up short.

"O Patrick Raftery, Ireland's Wonder!" he shouted.

Raftery and Hilaria and the shaggy wolf-dog stood still.

"England's Envy," went on the farmer, "and the Delight of the World!"

"I grant you," Raftery smiled. "But what the devil is it all about?"

"Let you shout for your harp, and get to work immediately, for this is what is in it: old Ireland is free."

"What's happened, honest man?"

"Let you get to work, Patrick Raftery, and write a poem will rock the ages. O'Rourke," he whispered, "Prince of Breffni, is coming home from Portugal."

"O'Rourke is my cousin ; and I haven't heard of it."

"Don't I know O'Rourke is your cousin?

Am I an ignorant man? Am n't I telling you?"

"You are not."

"'Tis this way, Patrick Raftery: the Welshman of Claregalway has sold back Breffni to the O'Rourke, so as to get money to put in the South Sea scheme. 'Twas long he held out, but at last he's in it, up to the neck, begor. He sold it for next to nothing so as to get more money, to put in the hands of the South Sea merchants. And isn't it in the prophecies of Columkill, Patrick Raftery, that the old princes will come back and the foreigners leave the country? And a woman will walk in the sea from Aran to the mainland, and a miller without thumbs will appear in the county of Louth?

"Sure the cliffs are lined with people ten deep waiting to see the women walk on the waters. And isn't Joey Persse gone on his racing horse to the county of Louth, to hear tell did e'er a one lay eyes on a miller without thumbs?

"Let you get down to your work now, Patrick Raftery, and be losing no time at it, for fear Ireland might be free before you're ready, and they'll be asking you for a poem on it, and you'll be shamed before the nations of the world, and the great poetic Irish nation!"

CHAPTER XI

Outside the grey-turreted stronghold the breath of autumn filled the air with a fine frosty mist. All August that year had been heavy with produce, and now it was delivered of brown nut and russet apple. The grass was crisp, the roads shining as pewter. Orange and red the trees flaunted that were soon to be bare under the cold Irish winds. And everywhere was the perfume of the peat smoke, and everywhere the glossy busy crow. The sweet hush of autumn was in the trees, like a child breathing in its sleep.

Within the state room of Breffni were gathered from near and far the clans and families to welcome back the O'Rourke from Portugal. Though evening had not set in, the hall would have been dark but for the flaming torches on the wall. In the fireplace, wide as a gate, peat glowed and logs of bog-oak crackled. Everywhere underfoot were clean fragrant rushes, while on the walls the rosy Saracen carpets glowed in a sunset of soft colour. And here and there was a torn battle-flag, and here a drum splashed with the blood of the player who had drummed the O'Rourkes over the lead-swept plains of Low Germany with Wallenstein. And here in a corner, standing as a statue stands, was the figurehead of a Spanish admiral's ship, which the O'Rourkes had captured when the great Armada went forth. Everywhere in futile savagery grinned the heads of beasts O'Rourkes had hunted and killed, the great grey wolf and the vast bear.

Around the walls the guests of O'Rourke stood or sat silently, Irish gentlemen dressed according to their station and travel. Here one in the brocade and fashion of London, here an old chief in kilt and broadsword, here the wig of the Dublin beau, here the luxuriant uncovered locks of tradition. And everywhere the gentle Irish ladies, some with hair of red gold and eyes of yellow gold, and some with black hair and grey lovely eyes, and some with hair fair as flax and with eyes the soft blue of forget-me-nots. All tense and silent they listened as Raftery swept the strings of the Queen of Harps. Even the wolf-dog before the fire listened, fierce and eager, as the flying peremptory notes summoned **the** clansmen:

"I call from the shadow world
Guests of an ancient day:
O'Rourkes whose banner unfurled
In the breeze of Dublin Bay,
When the Tolka's waves ran red
With the blood of the routed Danes;
And Boru, the King," [the harp wailed], "lay **dead—**"

His head in the soft glow of the torches rose from the snowy collar, like the head of a new king on a new coin, so firm, so hawk-like, so purposeful; his beautiful well-kept hand flashed to and fro over the strings of the harp, the white and blue and golden and red strings. Behind him the gillie stood harsh-faced, on guard like a sentry.

"They come with sword and shield,
Down the lane of forgotten years,
Whence they sleep, on a foreign field.
For death cannot seal their ears
Against the old nostalgic lure
Of the harp they have not heard,
Since the trumpets of Agincourt—"

Through the dim hall an eerie sense crept that among them were shades of the giants of ancient days, great men in chain-mail and

fierce moustaches; knights in armour, esquires
with their hair cut in fringes over wide boyish
eyes. The smoke of the torches eddied and
took on shapes under the high black roof.
And suddenly, as the note of the harp died
away, a wolf-dog raised its head and belled
a great cry.

"Hush, little brother, hush!" called Raftery.

"O'Rourkes who stood by the line" [went on the song],
    "Of the archers plying their art,
  In sullen Palestine,
    With Richard the Lionheart!
  O'Rourkes who fought with the Maid
    In the flame of the battle ring,
  When the fair land of France was afraid
    Before the might of the English king."

The proud necromantic notes of the harp
faded into a soft gentle thrumming, that now
gave the humming of the bees in gardens, of
the whisper of flowers in the little breeze of
sunrise. Raftery's voice turned to a soft
murmur:

"And about us now are the dim fragrant women
    Who pledged their hearts on an altar,
  For fealty from O'Rourke and O'Rourke's yeomen:
    Hedda, the Norse viking's daughter.
  And that vivid Latin flame,
    Alois from Angoulême.

And she who was so bonny, and so good
    That in famine time she sold her rings
So even the wandering beggar might not want—
    The Hessian princess Ermintrude,
With brown hair close to her small nut-shapen head,
    All, all are here to-day," [he murmured], "although
        dead.

"To-day under this ivied generous pile " [the harp gave
        forth short pleading notes, as though in argu-
        ment]——
  "I would not refuse domicile
Even to her who forgot her marriage vows,
And the unspotted banner of this house,
Fleeing with her lover on a swift horse
While the Lord O'Rourke was at the pagan wars,
And when he returned on a broad bellying wind
    Cared nothing for the savage pain that tore him
    When the valley lay smiling before him
    Where lately he left her behind.

"One who is here to-day," [there came a throbbing deep
        note into the melody], "I wish most to praise
    Of all the great women who came to Breffni,
She crossed in inimical days,
    Fair English Daphne!
From Yorkshire's furthermost part.
    Her hair was yellow as primroses,
Her eyes sea-blue as when day closes,
    And warm and white and silken was her hand.
Yet not for these does her heart dwell in my heart,
    But for this, though English, she loved Ireland."

As he spoke on, the harp seemed more like a living thing he was controlling, as a man controls a great horse, than an instrument of red sally-wood and tuneful strings. It exulted in his every phrase as a salmon exults in the swift rapids of a river. Now its music curveted proudly to the glamour of fighting names; now it murmured reverently as he named the dim fragrant women of the house, fragrant as verbena; now it roared as he spoke of the winds that swept the battlements of Breffni; now it quivered as quivers the green garment of ivy on the wall of an old house when the southern wind is blowing. It changed to a tune merry as a piper's.

"Now for this
   Day I proclaim armistice!
Foemen shall forgive foeman;
   And there shall be love between men and women.
O'Rourke's noble feast
   Shall ne'er be forgot.
No sportsman shall chase the game beast;
   Or angler kill the fish-poaching stoat;
The hare may canter the grassy fields;
   And birds take their tithe of what the harvest yields,
And the red dog-fox may emerge from the spinney—
   Playraca na Roorka,
   I givna gahan dhinny !"

BLIND RAFTERY

A wolf-hound walked over solemnly and laid its great head on Raftery's knee, looking up at him with brown wonder in its eyes. The gillie stirred to move it, but Raftery called, "Let him be!" and shifted the harp.

"The green banner cracks on the towers," [he went on],
   "And all our small brethren make holiday—
The bee in the mistletoed bowers;
   The sleek mouseen in the acres of hay:
Through the woods unafraid stalks the timid pheasant,
   And in the meadows the stallions whinny—
Every peasant
   Has his butter-coloured guinea.
Playraca na Roorka," [he swept the strings],
"*I givna gahan dhinny!*"

He let the gay sonorous notes die off, and suddenly began plucking a swift lamenting little melody on the minor strings. He raised his bronze face toward the flare of the torches, and there were lines of pain about his mouth:

"Querulous old men say
   Nothing remains;
Everything wonderful melts away,
   As snow before rains.
Many an ancient house
   Has had its end,

And the morose grouse
    Is the only friend
To wander about and complain,
    Under grey autumn skies:
The friends of King Charlemagne—
    Even their memory dies!"

A chill winter atmosphere came into the room, a chill as of an oak wood in midwinter with the snow upon the ground, and only the melancholy daw in the bare branches. A wolf-bitch cried softly by the fire, and her mate moved closer to her protectingly. The bass strings of the harp pealed like an organ.

"Though much of our greatness die
    From Derry to Cork,
  Yet this I prophecy:
    That Clan O'Rourke
Shall remain in the Irish land,
    Honoured and proud,
While the constellations stand,
    Until, on a silver cloud,
Christ comes in majesty
    To proclaim the end of all things,
And the stars bow down in the sky,
    And the sun sings."

His hands dropped from the harp, and he sat there for a moment tired, repeating to himself the phrase: "*Playraca na Roorka,*

O'Rourke's noble feast, *I givna gahan dhinny*, shall ne'er be forgot." And suddenly from all in the house went up a great shout, that was taken up by those outside until the whole country rang with cheering, and even the walls of Breffni shook, and the harp murmured to the deep vibration. O'Rourke's wife ran forward to him, with tears in her eyes, and kneeling beside him took his hands. She was a rounded sweet woman, with a great heart.

"O cousin Patrick Raftery," she said, "what can we do, what can I do, to make up to you for a poem like that?"

"My dear," he said, "it was nothing but one of the house boasting to the length and breadth of Ireland."

O'Rourke himself, Rory More, Great Rory as he was called, came up in his shy childlike way. He was a huge figure, broad and muscular, and very little short of seven feet tall. He was reputed to be the best swordsman in Europe: but whether this was due to his great reach, and fastness like a cat's, or to deep skill with the weapon, has never been quite decided, though nights have been spent and blood let in arguing it. He was a silent, seemingly awkward man, with a slow patient smile.

"Patrick," O'Rourke's wife pleaded, "let us have the honour of making you some gift for the great poet you are."

"I may not be a great poet at all, Nora," Raftery smiled, "for we of the Irish nation have a bad habit of overrating ourselves. But, Cousin Nora, am I not an Irish gentleman?"

"O Patrick Raftery," she answered, "not even O'Rourke, Prince of Breffni, is a truer Irish gentleman."

"I should like to hear that contradicted," growled O'Rourke.

"Cousin Nora," Raftery said, "I have a wife, Hilaria, who is very shy, and would not come here. She is at the village inn, Cousin Nora. Will you ask her to come here?"

O'Rourke's wife's sweet face became white and frightened. She cast a quick glance at her husband. O'Rourke's face lit up with all his quiet grim fighting smile. He nodded to her.

"Of course, Cousin Patrick," she said and rose. She put her hand for an instant kindly on the silvering curly hair. "Of course!"

"Pat," O'Rourke growled, "you're a great lad. I don't know much about poetry, but I know this: you're a grand fellow. It's often

BLIND RAFTERY

I've spoken about you to the king of Portugal and the king of Spain when they've been trotting out their fancy poets. I've told them, 'I've a cousin in Ireland, Patrick Raftery, the chief Irish poet, would take that fellow like a beagle takes a hare.' Queer enough," he said, and he shifted the heavy sword-belt, "I never found anyone to contradict me, so they must have heard of you over there already."

"Rory More," Raftery told him, "you're the world's liar and a bloody ruffian."

"I am not, Pat," he protested indignantly; "they have heard of you—from the moment I began talking, they admitted you were the better man."

He walked across the rush-strewn floor abruptly, the long Spanish rapier slapping against his knees as he walked. Suddenly the gillie sprang in front of Raftery.

"What is the matter, fool?" Raftery asked.

"Master," the gillie answered, "keep close to the wall, and give my arm room. There is going to be fighting here."

"As how?"

"O'Rourke has taken the leaders of the clans aside and is talking to them at the end of the long room. They are growling and have black faces."

"Yes?"

"O'Rourke is smiling," the gillie reported, "and he has drawn his great sword. And now the growling has ceased."

"Go on, boy!"

"O'Rourke has sheathed his sword."

Raftery sensed that the gillie was trembling as a sensitive hunting-dog trembles. He put out his hand and gripped the boy's arm.

"Well?"

"The Lady Nora has come in," he said, "and with her, sir, is my mistress Hilaria."

"Yes, boy?"

"O'Rourke has drawn his sword again and is walking toward them."

Raftery said nothing, but his grip tightened on the boy's arm.

"O master," said the gillie wonderingly, "great O'Rourke has dropped on his knees, and is kissing my mistress Hilaria's small hand."

CHAPTER XII

ABOVE their heads, on this splendid winter night, a huge primrose-coloured moon hung, and on the edges of the sky were the faint spangles of stars. The road was black, except for here and there a patch of white hoar-frost. To the right and left of them were the wide plains of Meath. The grass was stiff with frost; the little groves of birch-trees were silent in the windless night. Only the whistle of the snipe was heard, and the booming of the bittern from some distant bog. They had been riding all day on their way from Dublin to Connaught and were looking forward to seeing the first lights of Mullingar. There they would rest for the night, and in the minds of Raftery and Hilaria was the pleasant picture of the inn. The cheery housemaids rushing with steaming water for their baths, the rosy landlord lumbering about for his best Belfast linen and putting candles of white bee's-

wax into sticks of polished brass, and seeing that
the fires were burning briskly in their rooms.
And all the house would be in a bustle when
they knew who the guests for the night were,
the roar in the kitchen, the rush to the cellar
for the most cobwebbed bottle of choice wine.

The clamour of the capital city was still in
their ears. The shouts that had greeted
Raftery when he appeared in the streets.
The great reception in the Irish House of
Commons and in the Irish House of Lords,
where, before each, he had played on the
harp, reciting "The Green Woods of Truagh"
and "County Mayo," and his great new poem,
the "Dhrinnan Donn"—"The Flowering of
the Hawthorn-Tree"—in praise of Hilaria.
In the theatre in Fishamble Lane the play
was not allowed to go on until Raftery had
been helped on the stage and given a poem to
the people. Everywhere was gaiety in Dublin
where in London was poverty and desolation,
for the immense South Sea Bubble had broken,
and every English home had suffered, where
Ireland was little affected, if at all. So the
sweet Irish ladies went to the theatres and
balls preceded by their small negro pages with
torches, and the great adventurers from the
continental wars ruffled along Bachelors' Walk,

and the Irish peers rumbled into the capital in their huge coaches. And all, all gave homage to blind Raftery.

The ring of the sharpened shoes on the frosty road clinked in the air. Beside Raftery Hilaria rode on the splendid Spanish mule he had bought for her in Dublin. She was enveloped in a huge frieze driving-coat he had made her put over her Irish cloak, and only the tip of her white childish face was visible. Her foot in its riding-boot of green leather rested like a feather in the stirrup. Raftery's great cloak was wrapped about him against the chill air. A hundred yards behind trudged the gillie with the packhorse and the wolf-hound. His plaid was gathered about him, and he was humming to himself a poem that had been composed by some penny poet or come-all-ye singer of Dublin in praise of Raftery, "*Noora hogan Parig Raftara Kondha Weeo*," "When Patrick Raftery Raises the County of Mayo." The breaths of Raftery and Hilaria turned into silver funnels of frost in the keen air.

From a coppice on the side of a road a beggar shambled forward. He had an old hat on, and an ancient swallowtail coat swept the ground behind him as he limped with the cold.

"Irish nobles," he whined, "give alms to

one who has been a godly man and a merchant of substance in his day. I am not an ordinary beggar. I was at ease," went the sancti-monious plea, "but He hath broken me asunder; He hath also taken me by my neck, and shaken me to pieces, and set me up for His mark. I am a godly man, Irish nobles, but the ill-living merchants of London caught me in their South Sea snare."

Raftery felt about him, and remembered there was a pocketful of guineas in his frieze greatcoat.

"Hilaria," he said, "give alms to the Welshman of Claregalway."

There was a chink of gold pieces thrown on the hard black road. They did not stop. The hoofs of the horses rang out like the blows of little hammers. Above them hung the honey-coloured moon. Before them rose dimly the lights of Mullingar, where soon there would be immense pleasant bustle when they dis-mounted before the principal inn. Behind them the gillie broke into the crude street song:

"In all this mighty nation there is great admiration,
    And loud appreciation from Howth to Killaloe;
    And such gigantic praises were never heard, by Jasus!
    As when Patrick Raftery raises the County of Mayo
    Noora hogan Parig Raftara Kondha Weeo!"